.75

"Sixteen-year-old Kim Andrews is obsessed by questions about her father, Kenji Yogushi, who died before she was born. Secure in the love of her Irish-American mother, stepfather, and little half brother, Kim still needs to find out about her lost heritage. The girl goes to San Diego in search of the Yogushis, despite her mother's sad report that they disowned Kenji for marrying against his father's wishes. Kim meets hospitable Japanese-Americans as she carries on her mission and learns how they and their families—all loyal American citizens—were imprisoned during World War II, after the attack on Pearl Harbor. Gaining understanding of Nisei customs and the injustices endured by her father's people, Kim fears but forces herself to meet with his mother and aunt, climaxing in a drama that Irwin spices with naturally amusing episodes."

—*Publishers Weekly*

KIM/KIMI

KIM/KIMI
Hadley Irwin

Puffin Books

PUFFIN BOOKS

A Division of Penguin Books USA Inc.
375 Hudson Street, New York, New York 10014
Penguin Books Ltd, 27 Wrights Lane, London W8 5TZ, England
Penguin Books Australia Ltd, Ringwood, Victoria, Australia
Penguin Books Canada Ltd, 10 Alcorn Avenue, Toronto, Ontario, Canada M4V 3B2
Penguin Books (N.Z.) Ltd, 182–190 Wairau Road, Auckland 10, New Zealand

Penguin Books Ltd, Registered Offices: Harmondsworth, Middlesex, England

First published in the United States of America
by Margaret K. McElderry Books/Macmillan Publishing Company, 1987
Published in Puffin Books 1988

17

This novel is a work of fiction. Any references to historical
events; to real people, living or dead; or to real locales are
intended only to give the fiction a setting in historical reality.

Library of Congress Cataloging in Publication Data
Irwin, Hadley.   Kim/Kimi by Hadley Irwin.   p. cm.   "Puffin books."
Summary: Despite a warm relationship with her mother, stepfather,
and half brother, sixteen-year-old Kim feels the need to find
answers about the Japanese American father she never knew.
ISBN 0-14-032593-X
{1. Identity—Fiction.   2. Japanese Americans—Fiction.   3. World
War, 1939–1945—Evacuation of civilians—Fiction.   4. Fathers and
daughters—Fiction.}   I. Title.
PZ7.I712Ki 1988   {Fic}—dc19   88-17268   CIP

Printed in the United States of America
Set in Garamond #3

For Barbara Hiura and Ernie Pons,
who shared their lives with us

KIM/KIMI

ONE

"I don't understand you." Principal Sturm folded her hands into a ball of fingers and peered at me over the top of her half glasses as if she had two sets of eyes.

I looked out the window. It was April. The maples on Second Street were budding, and the sun filtered down through branches upon patches of new green. It reminded me of the opening paragraph of my favorite book, *Candi for Bart*. I had just finished reading it yesterday—for the twelfth time.

> *Candi felt the April breeze ruffle her soft blond hair and smiled. Friday afternoon and soon she'd be meeting Bart—her Bart. She thought of his warm hazel eyes flecked with gold and smiled again. She walked faster. She didn't want to make him wait.*

"You've been tardy six times. Absent five days. Your grades are a disgrace, and now Mr. Mitchell tells me you walked out of his history class. Why, Kim?"

I glanced back at Miss Sturm. She was still looking at me. I avoided her eyes by staring down at the name plate on her desk: INEZ STURM, PRINCIPAL. I wondered if they ever called her *Nez* when she was a kid, if she ever was a kid.

"Why, Kim?" She leaned toward me. When principals lean across the desk, you'd better find an answer.

I looked around the room. Miss Sturm had shelves of books all over her office, from floor to ceiling. Teachers and principals must think books make a good impression. Nez couldn't have gone through all of them, even if she read one book every day. Though her hair did have little sprinkles of gray around the edges, she really didn't look that old. But maybe she had read them all.

"Why, Kim?" she repeated.

"Because . . . ," I began.

"Because is not an answer, Kim."

I wanted to tell her that *why* was not a question, but you can't say things like that when you're on the wrong side of a principal's desk. I smiled instead. When you smile, no one knows what you're really thinking. I had smiled a lot that year.

"You were such a fine student your sophomore year." She leaned back in her chair. "But for now, let's forget about all those other things. What happened today in Mr. Mitchell's class? Why did you walk out?"

I tried to look at her again, but it was hard. Miss Sturm

shaved her eyebrows and painted them back on, so she always looked surprised. I bet she even looked surprised when she was sleeping.

"I'm waiting for an answer, Kim."

"Why?" I repeated. I could see the word in big capital letters. It was a funny word, really, but it had a nice sound—like a breeze through grass, if you didn't think of what it meant. I decided I'd better try to tell the truth.

"Mr. Mitchell was showing a film. I'd seen it four different times in junior high!"

"Oh." Miss Sturm's mouth looked as surprised as her eyebrows. "Well, then, why didn't you explain? You could have asked for a pass to the library."

"I didn't want to interrupt the movie."

That was *not* the truth, and somehow Miss Sturm knew it. I had been reading *Heart of Love* when the film began.

> *Steve leaned casually against a locker, his blue eyes smiling. "So how about it, Cindy, would you go with me to the movie Saturday?" She hoped she wasn't blushing. Steve, the most popular boy in school, a senior, was asking her for a date. She smiled up at him and nodded.*

Miss Sturm chewed on the edge of her thumb for a minute, then reached for the phone. "I think, Kim, I'd better have your mother come in to see me."

She must have known our number by heart because she didn't even bother to look for the phone book.

"Nobody's home," I hurried to explain, telling the truth again. "They went to Chicago for a week. They left this morning."

"You're not staying alone!" Miss Sturm almost lost her eyebrows under her bangs.

"Oh, no. Davey and I are going to stay with Mrs. Mueller."

"Oooh." Her voice went like a roller coaster, up and down and up again. "Well. . . ." She chewed on her thumb. "You'd better take a note home and have your mother call me when she gets back. Of course, next week is spring vacation. . . ." She consulted a calendar. "But the Monday after." She pulled an orange slip from a tall stack, scribbled on it, and handed it to me.

I started for the door.

"And, Kim, I want you to think through your problems. After all, you're sixteen, old enough to be responsible. Think carefully about what *you* can do to improve your attitude."

I stuffed the orange slip into my purse and rushed out the door. How could she expect me to think about my problems when I was already late for trig? Class was half over, but at least it was the last period of the day.

"Hey, Kim! Mitchell nail you for skipping class?" Spider Jenkins came loping down the hall.

All you could see when you looked at Spider were arms and legs and hair, which went only one way, up, no matter how he tried to smooth it down. Together we looked like

6

Tiny Alice and the Snark. This wasn't at all like *A Guy for Gina.*

> *Gina heard footsteps behind her as she hurried down the hall. Before he spoke, she knew it must be Greg. How could she let him down gently? Oh, sure, they'd dated for a while and he was handsome and rich and captain of the track team, but he didn't make her pulse race the way Andy did.*

"Of course he nailed me. What else is new?"

"He got me, too. Wasn't doing nothing neither. Honest. Just trying to get my books out of my locker, you know, and this guy comes along, you know, and gives me the elbow."

"Don't tell me," I muttered. "Tell Sturm."

Spider's record for detentions and visits to Sturm's office almost equaled mine. Not that he did anything on purpose. Things just happened.

"How come you walked out on Mitchell?"

"I'd seen the dumb film before. A hundred times!"

"Me too. Bombs and all that junk. Mom goes crazy when they show stuff like that on TV. She's Quaker."

I wasn't interested in Spider's family and what they liked.

"Can't blame her, though. Her brother served in the Navy, you know. Kamikaze got him."

The turkey! Couldn't he see I was half Japanese and ready to scream?

"How's the Big Nez?" He motioned toward the office door. "In a good mood?"

"The usual. Biting her thumbnails."

"It figures. Well. . . ." He took a big breath and pushed on the office door. "Here we go again, Inez."

The Kamikaze thing did it! I was *not* going to trig. I had an A going anyway—my only A. Instead I'd do what Sturm suggested. I'd think about my problems, and I certainly couldn't do that in trigonometry. My problems weren't something simple like that. Math questions had answers.

With Eagle Eye Sturm locked in with Spider, I walked slowly down the hall, through the side door, and out to the parking lot. It wasn't the first time I'd slipped out last period. It was simple. All you had to do was pretend you had permission. Once I walked out past Mr. Mitchell, and he didn't even notice me.

Jav's *Pink Passion* was where I thought it would be, jammed into the chain-link fence in the far corner. Jav could have had any car she wanted—her parents owned half the town—but the *Passion* was something special: a 1954 Buick, fuchsia on the bottom, white on top, with four circles that looked like portholes on either side of the hood. Her dad collected antique cars, and after a lot of persuading, he had let her have this one for her own.

I climbed into the backseat, propped my head against the armrest, my feet against the window. Jav had French last period. She always met me after school with new

French phrases she had made up in class. I'm not sure they meant anything, but they sounded sexy.

I reached into my book bag and pulled out my newest teen romance: *Lovely But Lonely.* Mom threatened to cut off my allowance if I kept on buying such books, but she should have been glad I wasn't drinking or doing drugs. I kept my books out of sight on the top shelf of my closet. Mom said it was the only tidy place in my entire room. Some of the books were pretty tattered, though, because I'd read them so many times; in fact, a lot of them I knew by heart. It was handy, really, because almost any time I wanted to I could switch out of what was going on around me and be right in the middle of a romance. It was like having a hearing aid that I could turn off and on. It solved a lot of problems.

"It is a problem." Green-eyed, red-haired Julie nodded her head sympathetically. "It's not your fault you're so popular, Lisa, but you can't go to the same dance with both Ted and Jerry."

I was glad Mom wasn't home. At least she'd be spared another orange slip from Nez. Mom always looked sort of helpless when she read one. I dug down into my purse. The slips usually said the same thing, only in different words like "does not apply herself." It sounded like the directions on a glue bottle. Jav thought "lacks effective self-motivation" had a nice ring to it.

I uncrumpled the slip.

Dear Mrs. Andrews:
Please call after spring vacation in reference to your
daughter Kim and her school citizenship.

What if Nez deprived me of my citizenship? She could.
She would, too. Nez had a heart lined with fangs.

Below was a printed multiple-choice list of no-no's
decorated by Nez checks:

> *does not associate with peers*
> ✔ *is not goal-oriented*

Nez knew more about goals than our football team.

> *is disruptive*
> ✔ *ignores rules*
> *negligent with assigned work*

She'd have checked that, too, if she'd known I hadn't
even started my history paper for Mitchell, and it was due
the week after spring break.

> ✔ *displays inconsistent behavior*
> *is unattentive*
> ✔ *is uninterested*
> ✔ *lacks accountability*
> ✔ *needs behavior modification*
> *lacks cognitive skills*

I stuffed the slip back into my purse. I thought briefly about throwing it away, hoping by the time spring vacation was over, Sturm would have forgotten about me. Unlikely. Principals are especially good about remembering what students want to forget.

It would mean another private talk with Mom, but nothing would change. We'd both feel uncomfortable. We'd both say the usual things, and Mom would end up shaking her head, and I'd make a promise I didn't really mean and wouldn't keep.

It hadn't always been that way. When I was a little kid in grade school, I could hardly wait to get home and tell Mom everything that had happened that day. We'd sit in the kitchen, and Mom would listen and laugh or look serious, depending on what I was saying. It was as if she were my best friend and there was nothing I couldn't tell her and she always understood.

I don't know why that stopped, exactly, but I guess it must have been in sixth grade. Heidi Hansen wanted me to give her my answers on a geography test, and I wouldn't do it. When the teacher wasn't looking, she leaned across the aisle and whispered "dirty Jap." She didn't say it loudly enough for anyone else to hear, but she might as well have shouted it. At first I didn't know what she meant. Of course, I didn't look like the other kids in school, but I'd never thought much about that before.

When I got home, I didn't tell Mom about it. I pretended I had homework to do. From then on, I didn't tell

Mom a lot of things, and it got to be a habit. That's also when I started reading romances. At first they kind of reminded me of Mom's old schoolbooks—about a couple of kids named Dick and Jane. It was a familiar world where all the people were the same and there weren't any problems except for having to watch Puff, the cat, and Spot, the dog, run.

Run! I sat up straight in the backseat and stared out at the parking lot. Run! I'd do it. Just like good old Spot. Or like Angie, in *Running to Paradise*, who ended up engaged to her college track coach, except my reason for running was a whole lot better than hers.

I was going to run! I really was! I had been planning for a long, long time. I'd tried before—twice really. When I was fourteen, I got as far as the bus station, but Jav talked me out of it. Then last summer I was going to hitchhike, but I got scared and went back home. Nobody ever knew about that. When everything's screwed up and you're all tangled inside, what's there to do but run? I was a mixed-up kid any way I looked at it. I didn't like myself much; in fact, to tell the truth, I was probably the most boring person I knew, not at all like the people in stories. Jav kept telling me adolescence was only a disease and eventually I'd get over it, but "eventually" was so long in the future I couldn't begin to think that far.

I was a misfit, but there had to be some place where a misfit could fit, and that was what I was going to find. For sure, it wasn't in Lanesport, scrunched between Iowa hills and the Mississippi. In some ways, I suppose, I had about anything anyone could ever want. Mom and Dad were great, and Davey was a really super little brother, but I didn't belong . . . even in my family. I faked a lot. I mean, I tried to be like everybody else and to pretend it didn't matter, but it did. I had almost talked myself into what Jav called a "flamingo funk" when she opened the car door.

"How'd you get out here so fast? And what are you doing hiding in the backseat?"

"I skipped last period," I mumbled, climbing over into the front seat. "I've got to talk to you, Jav."

"What now?" Jav coaxed the *Pink Passion* to life, revved the motor, and backed up in a scream of white-walls, without once looking to see where she was going.

"Got sent up to Sturm."

"Not again! Why don't you ask if you can use her office for homeroom? Think of the time you'd save."

I didn't bother to answer. Jav wouldn't have heard me anyway. She was concentrating on avoiding kids and bicycles and school buses. The *Pink Passion* didn't have power steering, and it took all Jav's muscle to wheel the car through traffic.

"Got to fill up with gas first. This monster sucks it up like osmosis, even in the parking lot. Then we'll cruise around. See what's up."

I didn't want to cruise around. I wanted to talk. Cruising with Jav was like playing Russian roulette. You never knew which turn would produce the fatal bullet. That's why her father gave her the car in the first place. It was as safe as an armored tank with a front bumper that sprouted two chunks of metal that looked like battering rams so that every other driver on the road kept out of her way.

"Let's take the river road," I suggested.

"That kind of day?" Jav looked down at me and up just in time to negotiate an abrupt right-angled turn into the gas station.

Jav always looked down on me. She looked down on almost everyone from her six feet. Maybe some girls would have been unhappy being that tall, but not Jav. She loved it, and it showed. She wasn't beautiful, particularly, but she was what Mom called "striking." Of course, she was on the basketball team, had won every tennis championship in the state, and had collected so many track medals she used them to decorate the interior of the *Passion*, so that riding with Jav was like hearing wind chimes on every turn.

We managed to get out of the gas station without arguing about who would pay. I gave up when Jav explained that it was merely a simple process of converting plastic into fuel. "Dad says," she told me, "that's the only way I'll ever be financially solvent—letting credit card companies do my accounting."

"Javanita," I began, firmly.

Jav swung the car out into traffic without looking, amid a chorus of car horns from behind. "Is it that heavy?"

"That heavy," I repeated. "I want to ask a favor."

"No, you can't borrow my new sweater. It'd come down to your knees."

It was an old joke between us, but a comfortable one. It started because we knew how funny we looked walking down the halls together, Jav towering over me by a good foot. Maybe we laughed about it before anyone else could. We became friends back in junior high in phys ed class. I was always the last one chosen for volleyball or basketball or softball, and Jav, of course, the first. "If you get Jav, you have to take Kim."

I became Jav's handicap.

Jav became my best friend.

"Okay. Let's hear the worst. You're planning on T. P.-ing Sturm's front yard, and you want me to help. It's a deal, but I could use a hamburger first."

"Be serious, Jav. This is important. I want to use you as an excuse."

"I've been used before. Never for an excuse, though. What's up?"

"I want to tell Mrs. Mueller that I'm staying with you this week."

"Perfectly reasonable. Brilliant, in fact, except Mom and Dad are dragging me off to Colorado for spring break. And Jeffrey's coming home from college with who knows what collection of freaks, and he's taking over the house.

He's harmless, of course, but the folks would never let you stay in the house with him. They think the age of reason is forty-five. Otherwise, your idea is fine."

"You don't get it. I don't want to stay at your house. I need an excuse *not* to stay with Mrs. Mueller."

"Oh, you mean a cover." She took her eyes off the road. A truck swerved past with a nasty honk and a dirty look from the driver.

"Get us out of here, Jav, and I'll try to explain. It's a long story."

We headed down to the river and turned off on a scenic drive. A barge steamed slowly upriver, leaving a trail of black smoke in the clear spring sky. Jav pulled the *Passion* into the parking lot and shut off the engine. It always amazed me. Jav was the perfect picture of coordination, but for some reason it was impossible for her to drive and think and talk at the same time.

"Okay. Let's have it." Jav leaned back in the seat. "You're going to throw a party while your folks are gone. You can borrow my tapes. You can even borrow brother Jeff and whoever he brings home. It'll keep him off the streets."

"I said this was serious, Jav."

"Okay. Serious."

"I'm going to California."

Jav reached up and straightened the row of track medals that hung down from the sun visor. "My folks are right.

Forty-five *is* the age of reason. You're off your perch, you know, running away."

"This is the perfect time."

"I know you've talked about it. Tried it once, too."

"Don't you see? No one will miss me. No one will even know I'm gone."

"You're going alone! You can't be serious. You don't even know where you're going. Oh, sure, Sacramento, but it's a big city and all you have is a name."

"And a picture," I reminded her.

"They may not even live there anymore. Can't you at least talk to your mom about it first? I mean when she gets home?"

"What's there to say? I've asked her a dozen times, and she's told me all she knows, I think. Anyway she doesn't like to talk about it. And she doesn't understand. It's not a part of her. It's a part of me . . . a part that's missing. I can't explain it. It's something I feel."

Jav toyed with the steering wheel. "You're coming back, aren't you?"

"Of course! I'm not running away from home. I'm going to find out something about me."

"But why now?" Jav sank into the seat. "And why sneak off?"

"I'm not sure. All I know is that this is the time."

Jav traced the circle of the steering wheel with one finger. "Something must have triggered it."

I breathed out and drew in a deep breath. "It was the movie in history class. I walked out."

"The Pearl Harbor thing?"

"The Pearl Harbor thing. You don't know what it's like—nobody knows what it's like—to sit through it. The kids staring at me as if I were someone they'd never seen before. At least that's the way it feels." I stopped. Jav did not answer.

It had happened every year since junior high whenever December 7 came around or anyone mentioned the attack on Pearl Harbor. There was no way I could deny being Japanese—half Japanese, that is, thanks to a father I'd never known. When I was born, I was Kimi Yogushi. When I was three and Mom remarried, I became Kim Andrews. I didn't know then that names and faces made such a difference, but after I got into junior high I found out. It wasn't so much that I didn't want to be Japanese—half Japanese. I didn't want to be different.

"Run away then. Go ahead. Be a missing person."

Sometimes Jav didn't act like my friend.

"It's just for one week!" I was almost yelling.

"It's stupid!" Jav turned to me. She was not smiling. "You run off, all by yourself, to find your father's family that your mother lost track of before you were born. It's dumb! What'll you find out? What good will it do you? Wait until you're eighteen. At least you will be legal then."

"You sound like Mom."

"What's this big deal about your real father. He's dead, isn't he?"

"Yes . . . but . . . ." I usually didn't have trouble explaining things to Jav. "He certainly had to have a family out there someplace."

"Oh, I agree. He must have had a family. Most people do."

Jav was being worse than nasty.

"You don't understand either!" I looked out at the river. The barge was almost out of sight around the farthest bend.

"What don't I understand?"

"Well, what am I supposed to be? I'm half and half. I look Japanese—"

"Look Japanese for me." Jav giggled.

I ignored her and went on. "Mom's pure Irish, so that makes me Irish-American on the inside and Japanese-American on the outside."

"Oh, quit acting adolescent. You think you're alone?" Jav stared down at the dashboard. "On the inside I'm five foot four, weigh 110, and everyone thinks I'm the cutest little thing they've ever seen. We all have an inside *me* and an outside *I*."

"Why not an inside *I* and an outside *me*?"

"Whatever."

"Being tall is not the same as being half and half."

"You sound as if you belong in a milk carton." Jav

shook her head. "I suppose the only way I can stop you is to do something sensible like calling your parents. Or mine. Or the police."

"You won't, though, will you?" I nudged her in the ribs.

"Probably not. You're going to do it someday, anyhow, but listen to me. If you go and anything bad happens to you, I'll break your face!"

I almost changed my mind then, because I *was* scared— not about going to California by myself, but about what I might find when I got there.

"You don't have to worry about me," I said with as much sureness as I could. "I'll keep in touch with Davey. He'll know where I am. We've got it all worked out. I've been planning it for a long time."

Jav looked at me as if I'd misplaced my marbles. "I must be the one who's crazy. How old's your little brother? Twelve? What can he do? And when is this big getaway?"

"Tomorrow, if you'll cover for me."

"Tomorrow! What's the rush?"

"It's as good a time as any, isn't it? You won't rat on me, will you?"

"Have I ever?" Jav reached for the ignition key.

She didn't talk on the way home. I tried to start a conversation a couple of times when she stopped for a traffic light, but it didn't do any good. The only thing she said, when I got out of the car, was, "Just remember, birdbrain, if you get kidnapped or murdered, I'll kill you! I really will!"

Davey was home, sitting at the kitchen table with a quart of milk and a stack of Oreos. He didn't look up when I came in because he was reading one of his dumb books, the kind with technicolor monsters and armored adventurers on the cover. I stood looking at him for a minute because I realized I wouldn't be seeing him for a while. In spite of what I'd told Jav, I really didn't know if I would go or when I'd be back, if I went.

Davey was, next to Jav, my favorite person, even if he was only twelve. Maybe it was because he looked like some elf out of one of the books he was always reading. His ears stuck out, his hair was sort of orange, his eyes green, and he should have been wearing the kind of shoes with toes turned up and little bells on them. Ever since he'd discovered fantasy games, he'd spent most of his time sketching maps of weird caves and sunken cities on graph paper.

I sat down beside him. The milk carton had pictures of two missing kids on it. I turned it so I couldn't see the faces. "I want the money," I said.

Davey peered up from his book as if he were swimming to the surface from one of his underground seas. "Now?"

"We started World War II in history class."

"Were you inscrutable?" Davey closed his book.

"Not very. I walked out."

"You walked out!" He sounded like Miss Sturm.

"I couldn't stand hearing one more time, 'A day that will live in infamy. Japs bomb Pearl Harbor in sneak attack.' I hate history, Davey. You just finish off one war, and you start another. And everyone looks at me as if World War II were my fault. This isn't 1941, is it? And I'm not a Jap. I'm an American. I can't take it anymore. I have to get out, Davey. I mean it."

"You mean you're really going to run away? You sure?" He had a little milk mustache on his upper lip, but he looked so grown up and serious that I didn't even try to wipe it off. "It'll be scary."

"I'm not running away! I'm going on a quest, remember? All quests are scary."

When I said "quest," his face brightened.

"Besides, we have it all planned. Like your Dungeons and Dragons."

"I know, but Dungeons and Dragons is pretend. This is real."

"Then pretend this is pretend." I reached out for one of his Oreos.

"That's hard! I can pretend something's real, but when something's *really* real, it's hard to pretend it's pretend."

"You're making my head hurt, Davey."

"You know what will happen if Mom and Dad find out."

"Sure. They'll ground me again."

"That'll be the third time this month!"

"Who keeps track?" I bit into my cookie. Davey was

wrong. Dad wouldn't just ground me. He'd grind me—into little pieces.

"I heard Dad tell Mom not to worry. That you were only going through a phase. You know—like those books you read all the time."

"You and your big ears," I snapped. "Just go get your Plan A."

There were times when I thought they should declare little brothers illegal.

I didn't need Davey's Plan A, and I didn't believe in his fantasy worlds, but it was a way to get him to help. Mrs. Mueller was responsible for his obsession. She had been our baby-sitter ever since she retired from teaching, and not just a baby-sitter for us, but for nearly every other kid in the neighborhood. Most of her sittees were in college now, but whenever they came home for vacation, they all gathered at her house for another round of Dungeons and Dragons.

Davey said playing the game was almost as good as reading a book because you got to be one of the characters and help make up the story. Almost everything in the game depended upon the roll of the dice to figure out what was going to happen. Mrs. Mueller was training Davey to be a Dungeon Master, the one who set up the scene and supplied the monsters.

Davey came up from the basement with his fishing-tackle box that he kept hidden behind Dad's workbench and unlocked it carefully as if it were a treasure chest.

"Now, remember," I warned. "You're not to tell any-one. This is *our* secret."

He looked up at me. "I made a vow of silence, didn't I?"

"Yes. But are you sure?"

"You can't break a vow. It's the rule of the game. Mrs. Mueller says so. Here's your ticket. *Our* money. Plan A." He spread out several sheets of graph paper Scotch-taped together. "We'd better go over it again from the begin-ning." He smoothed out the papers.

"Must we?" I knew the whole thing by heart. "We just went over it last month, remember?"

"You have to. I'm the Dungeon Master. That's the way you're supposed to do it. Anyway, I changed it a little."

"Hurry up, then. If I'm going, I've a lot of stuff to do."

"Okay." Davey sat up straighter, placed both hands on the table, palms down on each side of the paper and began. "The Sinister Secret of Sacra Mounto. Somewhere in the dark, winding streets of Sacra Mounto—"

"Oh, Davey, knock it off. We don't know the streets are dark and winding. You've never been there and neither have I."

Davey looked at me as if I'd cheated on a dice roll. "Just listen, will you?" He began to read again. "Some-where in the dark and winding streets of Sacra Mounto live the last descendants of a royal samurai warrior. Where they live, if they live, is the quest of Sybil the Seeker."

"Sybil the Seeker!" I tried not to laugh.

"That's new, Kim. I made it up. Do you like it? It's like a code name. No one but us will ever know."

"Sure. Sure. I'll be Sybil the Seeker. Go on, but hurry it up."

"Sybil the Seeker has but two clues to aid her in her quest: the name Yogushi (Sybil herself is a Yogushi) and a picture of her mother and the subject of this quest, her *real* father."

"I'm just half Yogushi, Davey."

"I know, only let's pretend you're all Yogushi. It makes it easier." He began to read again. "But before she can embark on her quest, Sybil must first escape from the clutches of the witch-monster Mueller—"

"That's not nice, calling Mrs. Mueller a witch-monster."

Davey ignored me. "—the clutches of the witch-monster Mueller. Then she must make her secret getaway from the haunted House of Andrew the Great—that's Dad." Davey stopped and cocked his head as if he were listening to something. "I can't figure it out. You're half Japanese and half not, and you're my half sister. That's three halves. Something's wrong."

"I know," I said. "That's the quest. To find the other half."

He looked up at me again. "If you find it, you won't change, will you?"

His question caught me in the middle of a swallow. "How would I change? You mean I might come back

25

wearing a kimono, eating with chopsticks, and spending my time arranging flowers? You're dumb, Davey. Plain dumb!"

"Okay. Okay. I just asked." He looked down at Plan A and then back at me as if he'd been caught rifling Mom's purse. "I made one change in the plan, though. You know your plane ticket? On open-booking? I bought you a round trip."

"What's the matter? Don't you trust me?"

"Sure." He grinned. "But a round trip's cheaper."

I wanted to hug him, but he was my brother.

TWO

Mrs. Mueller's door was never locked. Davey and I and everybody else knew we were supposed to walk in, stand in the hall, and shout. It was a big house with little rooms that branched off from halls on three floors and was as full of doors and surprises as any dungeon Davey could dream up. When I was little, the house frightened me.

"We're here," Davey shouted, his voice echoing up the stairwell.

"Third floor. Sunroom," came Mrs. Mueller's faint answer.

We never knew where we were going to find Mrs. Mueller. She didn't believe in hiring cleaning people. She said they invaded her privacy, so she did her own cleaning, one room per week. Whichever room she cleaned last became the "today" room. At first it had seemed funny to spend an afternoon sitting in a bedroom or the kitchen, but after a while we all got used to it because eventually all fourteen rooms became living rooms. The third floor sunroom was everyone's favorite.

Davey set his suitcase down. "Well . . . this is it," he said, looking up the long staircase. "You think we can fool her? She's awfully smart."

"Leave it to me," I said, pushing my bangs off my forehead. "I'll look her straight in the eye and tell her."

"I don't know. Do you think we really should?"

"We haven't been planning it all this time for you to back out, now that I've decided to go. Are you with me?" I started toward the stairs.

"Wait a minute. I just thought of something. If you're going tomorrow, you have to call the airline tonight and tell them you're coming so you'll have a seat."

"I will. Don't worry."

"I wish you'd change your mind, Kim." He sat down on the bottom step, his suitcase between his knees. "You should have asked Mom and Dad first. They might have let you go."

"Now listen, David Andrews! I'm not a child. I'm sixteen. I can take care of myself. I'll call you from Denver, when the plane stops over there, and every day after that. Mrs. Mueller won't know where I'm calling from and don't you tell her. I've got it all worked out." I started up the stairs . . . slowly. "Don't desert me now."

"Okay, Sybil. But don't blame me if something goes wrong."

"Come on!" I hissed through clenched teeth. "Don't be a poop-out!"

"I'm not." He stood up and brushed his hair from his forehead. "But I don't feel very good all of a sudden."

"Ave! Puer et puella!" Mrs. Mueller was sitting in her bamboo chair, the tall kind with a funny hood that draped over from the top. She had been a Latin teacher and insisted that reading a page from Virgil was as relaxing as an afternoon nap. No one really knew how old she was because, when her husband died, she started counting backwards on every birthday. "It's surprising," she told everyone, "how young it makes me feel."

"Hope you two didn't eat after school. I've been sitting here in a quandary and it hurts my back." She laughed. Mrs. Mueller often laughed at her own jokes whether anyone else did or not. "We're going to order pizza in and I can't decide whether to have the usual or the new combination of sauerkraut and Canadian bacon."

"Sauerkraut and bacon!" Davey shouted.

I could have kicked him. He wasn't thinking about Plan A. He was probably counting the extra pieces of pizza he'd get if I weren't around.

"And Davey." Mrs. Mueller put aside the book she had been reading. "Two new monster magazines came. I put them. . . ." She looked around the room. "Somewhere." Then she laughed again. "That'll be your first quest for the week. To find where I laid them down."

"Quest?" Davey looked at me as if Mrs. Mueller had discovered our entire Plan A.

"Go look for the magazines," I whispered and turned to Mrs. Mueller. "Why . . . ah . . . ," I began. Then I took a deep breath and began again, "Ah . . . Mom didn't have time to call you this morning before she left for Chicago, but I'm supposed to stay with Jav this week. Mom said so. I just walked over with Davey to tell you . . . I have to go back home and pack and—"

"Oh really! Well, that *is* nice." Mrs. Mueller smiled. Maybe she was relieved to have just one of us to take care of for the week.

"Javanita is such a fine young lady. She was one of my better Dungeon Masters. Too bad she grew out of it."

I glanced over at Davey who had *not* gone to look for the magazines. He shrugged. I tried again. "I promised Mom I'd call every day to check on Davey." I was having trouble looking at Mrs. Mueller. "We might be going out of town a couple of days . . . shopping . . . with Jav's folks . . . but I'll try to call before I leave. I wouldn't want Davey to get lonesome. I. . . ."

"Oh, don't worry about us. Davey and I have lots of things to do. And you and Jav come over. Anytime. You will, won't you, to see your brother?"

"Of course. I'll tell Jav." I was talking too fast. Then I remembered *The First Thursday*, a book about a fifteen-year-old girl named Thursday whose only flaw was that when she was embarrassed, she stuttered. All the boys thought it was cute, but it bothered her. She got over it by counting to three between words.

"And how is school, Kim? Are you still that excellent math student you always were? And you're into speech and dramatics too, I hear. But then I don't suppose you can tell about grades yet. It isn't report card time, is it?"

"No" . . . one, two, three . . . "But I'm doing" . . . one, two, three . . . "all right" . . . one, two, three . . . "I guess." I sounded as if I had the IQ of a weed.

"It's so important to learn as much as you possibly can when you're young. Do sit down for a minute, dear."

I sat down. This wasn't in Plan A, and Mrs. Mueller's minutes often turned into hours.

"I've just been reading about the Punic Wars."

Punic Wars. Maybe I could do my history paper on the Punic Wars, whatever they were.

"Have you covered them in your history class?"

"No." I squirmed farther back into the chair. "We're doing World Wars."

"Oh. World Wars. Much can be learned from history. I taught history too, you know," she went on. "Ancient history, that is."

I never knew how to carry on a conversation with someone who did all the talking, and Mrs. Mueller was that kind of someone. As for history, I considered it the armpit of the curriculum, but I smiled and said, "Is that so?" and wondered how I was going to escape.

"Ah, yes, history!" She gazed at the ceiling. "'The thought of our past years in me doth breed perpetual benediction.' That's Wordsworth."

I almost asked if he wrote in Latin, too, but I didn't. I smiled.

"You know, as I was sitting here reading just now, I got to thinking that our history was once someone's tomorrow. Isn't that fascinating?"

"Fascinating," I repeated in monotone. I glanced back at Davey. He shrugged and grinned.

"But enough of that." She stood up. "So you are going to stay with Javanita? Would you mind going past the post office? I have several letters that must go out today."

Mrs. Mueller made up crossword puzzles and acrostics for what she called "the Syndicate." Davey said it had something to do with newspapers, not the Mafia, and that she was paid money for it. I knew she received fan mail from all over. Davey claimed she knew people in every state from Maine to California.

"I'll be happy to mail them." Mrs. Mueller had no idea how happy I would be.

"Now you and Javanita have a wonderful time," she said, handing me the stack of letters.

"Oh, we will," I assured her, too eagerly. "And I'll check on Davey, and I hope he remembered to pack everything he needs, but I can bring it over tonight if he forgot anything."

Davey developed a sudden fit of coughing, and I stopped.

"I'm going down and bring up my stuff." He moved toward the door.

"You do that, Davey, and you might see if those magazines are down in the first-floor den." Mrs. Mueller sat down and readjusted her glasses.

"Well, good-bye, Mrs. Mueller, and thanks for taking care of Davey." I edged toward the door.

She looked up over her glasses, smiled, and picked up her book. "*Quo vadis? Via est asperrima.*"

She sounded as if she were talking to me instead of reading aloud in Latin.

"I think we muffed it," Davey whispered, taking two steps at a time down the stairs.

"Why?"

"You've never played Dungeons and Dragons with her. She smiles like that, and the first thing you know you're trapped in a bottomless pit on a deserted island."

"Oh, don't be a wimp! She believed me . . . I think."

"Want to bet? You've got to learn to lie better, Kim. Maybe it's not such a good plan after all," he muttered as he picked up his suitcase.

"You're not backing out on me, are you?"

"No, but when you really play Dungeons and Dragons, you take a band of people with you. You're going all by yourself. What if something happens to you? What would I do?"

"Listen, Davey, it's an adventure, remember? Exciting. And nobody will ever know, except you and me?" I squeezed his shoulder. "I'll be all right. You'll see."

"You'll come back, won't you?"

"Of course, you dope!"

I couldn't think of anything to say, and I couldn't say what I wanted to say, so I dashed out the door and ran, the cold April wind stinging my eyes.

I was turning down our block from the post office when I saw a flash of fuchsia out of the corner of my eye. What were Jav and the *Pink Passion* doing on Third Street? She lived on the other side of town. Usually, if she had errands or stuff to do after school, she took me along. I had to admit, though, I hadn't been much fun to be with that afternoon. Even Jav had said I was running away, and Davey called it sneaking off. They didn't understand that there were some things you had to do by yourself, and finding out about my real father was one.

As soon as I got home—and before I could change my mind—I called the airline to see if there was space available. There was.

Alone in an empty house is about as alone as you can get. It's a waiting kind of stillness where sofa, chairs, tables, pillows, magazines are all frozen in place. I couldn't sit still. I ran upstairs and dug my backpack from my closet. It was ready to go. I had packed it one day after school when I was so mad I didn't know what else to do. It was the day the school counselors decided to organize a minority club, only they called it a Heritage Club. In Lanesport, it was a very small group. I was already a minority. I didn't need a Heritage Club to tell me.

I checked again to see if I had remembered everything: a couple of pairs of Levis, sweater, a couple of shirts, a guide to the city of Sacramento. I counted my money again. The airplane ticket had exhausted my savings account. I had talked Mom into letting me draw out some money for a real cashmere sweater. I didn't tell her I drew out all my money that day. That and what I had managed to squirrel away from my allowance over the last several months had paid for my ticket, but I still had to borrow from Davey's savings, which he kept hidden in a strongbox in his bedroom, for money to live on when I was in Sacramento. I'd pay him back, though, someday. Pay him back double, even . . . maybe not quite double.

I had forgotten my books! I ran to the closet and peered up at the titles: *Desired Dreams, Sweet Memories, Cheers for Cathy, Born to Love, Second Love, A Lost Love.* I stuffed a bunch of them into my backpack, and grabbed another to read before I went to bed.

I went down to the kitchen, sat down at the table, and spread out Davey's Plan A.

1. *Flight leaves 8:45 A.M.*
    (A.M. *is morning*)
2. *Be at airport by 8*
    (*Be sure*)

I think Davey was born in a parenthesis!

3. *Don't miss the shuttle bus*
   (Catch it at Grand and 4th)

As if I didn't know.

4. *Stop at check-in counter. Get seat assignment and*
   boarding pass. Tickets made out to Kimi Yogushi
   (You are known as Sybil the Seeker only to me)
5. *Stop over in Denver*
   (Call from there for further instructions)
6. *Don't talk to strangers*
   (In a quest you have to be careful to find the true
   person behind the ugliest monster's disguise)
7. *In Sacramento, stay at the YWCA . . .*

I didn't have to go on. I had read it so many times, but down at the bottom of the last page, Davey had added something: *"If anyone discovers this plan, I hereby deny having prepared it except as an exercise in adventure planning for Dungeons and Dragons. (Signed) David A. Andrews."*

The toad! He'd be my partner, but if Mom and Dad found out it became all my doing. I wanted to run back over to Mrs. Mueller's, but then I had to laugh. Poor Davey had a hard enough time as it was convincing Mom and Dad that at twelve he was perfectly responsible and grown up.

THREE

I picked up *Stars for Steffie*, closed the blinds so neighbors would think no one was home, locked the doors, and headed for the rec room.

Nothing is harder than waiting for time to pass. It's bad enough at school if the class is boring and you're waiting for the bell to ring, but classes don't last for more than fifty minutes. I was stuck for the whole evening. I was lucky. I had Steffie and her stars—star quarterback, star debater, star-watcher—he was president of the astronomy club. I'd been saving the last chapter as a surprise for myself—and maybe for Steffie.

I didn't open the book right away. I was feeling a little guilty about lying to Mrs. Mueller. Mom and Dad had spent a lot of time teaching Davey and me to tell the truth at all costs, and most of the time I did, except when it cost too much. I sort of left things out, but I figured that wasn't really lying. It was just not telling the whole truth. Sometimes, though, you have to lie to make sense of the truth.

Jav says I don't really lie. I just "handle the truth with parsimonious frugality."

I could smell Dad's pipe tobacco in the humidor on the table beside me, and it didn't make me feel any better. He was a big, comfortable sort of man who looked more like a red-haired lumberjack than a professor. He was exactly the kind of person that anyone would want for a dad—funny and gentle and just strict enough to make Davey and me think twice before we did anything we knew was wrong—except for now. But now was different. I loved him because we were a family, and only when something came up like Pearl Harbor was I reminded that he wasn't my real father.

I wasn't sure, either, how I was going to explain this whole thing to him—or to Mom. If everything went right, they'd never know and I wouldn't have to explain. I wasn't running away from them. I was running toward something.

It all began to get to me when I was a freshman. Not that anything went wrong. I had plenty of friends. We had a gang that ran around together, had parties, did stuff, but when the boys started asking the girls to go to the drive-in or to a movie, no one ever asked me. Never! I couldn't figure out why. I laughed at everyone's jokes, even the ones that weren't funny. I smiled and giggled and joked, but no one, except Jav, ever seemed to want to be alone with just me. When you're fourteen, you begin to wonder what's wrong. It would have been better if I hadn't asked.

Davey looked at me as if my brains were mushed. "Don't you know why? You're different."

"What do you mean different?"

"Look in the mirror. You're Japanese."

"So what?"

"So you're different."

Do you know what it's like to look into a mirror and not look at all like the person you think you are? I tried make-up, and Mom let me get a curly perm and I read how to put on eye shadow. I'm not sure I looked any better, but I felt better. It didn't last long—neither did the perm. That's when I started wondering about my Japanese part.

"What was my real father like, Mom?"

We were sitting in the den that night. Davey and Dad were off on some Boy Scout overnight camp-out. Davey hated sleeping bags and tents and the outdoors in general, but he knew Dad loved the whole process, so he never argued about going.

Mom looked up and didn't answer right away.

"Besides being Japanese, I mean." That came out a little more sarcastically than I had meant it to.

"Japanese-American," she said, so softly that I almost didn't hear her. "I don't know what I can tell you that I haven't told you before, honey."

"Tell me again." I sounded like a whiney brat, but I'd spent half an hour in Miss Sturm's office that day, too. Even Jav hadn't been able to cheer me up.

"His name was Kenji. I met him when I was in college

39

in California. He was my professor. Older than I. He was killed in an accident before you were born. What more is there to tell? I came back here, met and married Daddy, and then Davey was born."

"I know that. But what was he like? Was he different, somehow, being Japanese?" It was a question I'd been thinking about a lot.

"It wasn't *what* he was that made him different—special. It was *who* he was." She closed her eyes for a minute, and when she spoke again it was as if her voice were coming from someplace far away. "Kenji was bright . . . beautiful . . . loving . . . gentle. He made my life exciting. How can I begin to tell you? I remember once we were walking along the beach, the wind blowing through his black hair, and he stopped, looked out over the ocean and said, as if he were lecturing the universe, 'Why are we so entangled in our past when now is such a miracle?' Kenji taught me the miracle of the now. Maybe that's why I've never talked much about him."

I couldn't believe what I was hearing! It was hard to imagine! My mother had actually been in love!

"Am I like him?"

"Oh, yes. In many ways. You're bright—beautiful—and sometimes silent. Your father could be silent, too. There were things your father would not—or could not—talk about . . . even to me. And you're headstrong, like him. It must be a family trait."

Somehow I'd never thought about my father having a family.

"But they're dead, aren't they?"

"I'm not sure. He had a sister. I never met her."

"But why don't you know? They'd be my family!"

"It's hard to explain, Kim."

"Was there something awful about his family?"

"No. Of course not. But his parents didn't approve of our marriage. They refused to meet me. You see, he was supposed to marry someone else. It had already been arranged."

"Arranged?"

"His father had chosen a Japanese girl. When Kenji disobeyed and married me, the family cut him out of their lives."

"Didn't you tell them about me?"

"I tried. I wrote to your grandparents when you were born. The letter came back."

"You mean I have a whole family I don't even know about?"

"I'm not sure." She stood up.

"It's all your fault." I knew that didn't make sense, but I couldn't stop the words.

"What's all my fault?"

"My not having a family."

She didn't bother to say that without her I wouldn't have been born at all. Instead she walked over, sat down, and put her arms around me. I wanted to push her away; then I was sure she felt the same hurt as I.

Still holding me, she smoothed my hair back as if I were a little girl. "There's a picture, Kim. I've kept it for you. Perhaps I've kept it too long. It's a wedding picture. Just a snapshot."

A picture and a name don't make a real father, but that was all I had. That was when I traded Heidi Hansen one of my books for her copy of *Runaway Love*, and that was when Plan A began.

It was almost dark when I went back upstairs to get something to eat. The phone rang louder than usual and kind of unfriendly, I didn't know whether to answer it or not. Certainly Mom and Dad wouldn't call here. They thought Davey and I were at Mrs. Mueller's.

"Hello, Melchior?"

It was Jav. All through grade school and even into junior high, Jav and I and Rita Mendez were always the three "Kings of Orient" in the annual Christmas program. I was a natural for Melchior, looking Oriental. Rita was a Chicano Balthazar, and Jav was Caspar because she was tall and could carry the tune. We all dreamed of some Christmas getting to be Mary. None of us made it. Heidi Hansen always beat us out. She was pretty and as blond as her name. When I got into high school we put on *The Mikado*, and I thought I was a shoo-in for Yum-Yum. Wrong! Heidi Hansen beat me out again.

"You aren't supposed to call me, Jav. I'm staying at your house, remember?"

"I'm not calling. I'm transmitting."

"What's the transmission?"

"Food! From hand to mouth to stomach. The parents went to the club. Jeff came home trailing trails of hunger and without any of those dweeby creatures that are usually attached to him. I'm starved. So . . . ?"

"When? Where?" At least it wouldn't be sauerkraut-and-Canadian-bacon pizza.

"Oh, in a few minutes. We'll pick you up. Unfortunately, there's no way I can get rid of the brother person, but if you're smart you'll put cotton in your ears and be enigmatic. See you."

I was halfway up the stairs to change into a clean pair of jeans when someone pounded on the back door. At first I thought maybe Davey had come back to pick up some more of his stuff. I struggled with the night lock.

"I didn't think anybody was home." Spider Jenkins filled the doorway.

"I was getting ready to leave."

Spider stuck both hands in his hip pockets and teetered back, almost falling off the top step. "Suppose I could borrow the front wheel off your bike? Sprocket's gone on mine. I'll have it back to you middle of the week. After the ride. Nobody's got one in town. Called all over. You know, you're the only kid I know that has a Japanese bike like mine."

"Japanese-American," I muttered.

"You going to be using yours?"

"No. I mean, I'm not going to be using it. And yes, sure. You can borrow the wheel. It's in the garage. Here, I'll show you."

I pushed him toward the garage, hoping Jav wouldn't mind waiting for me. "Just take the whole bike. Bring it back anytime. Next week."

"Don't need the whole thing. Just the wheel. I brought my tools with me."

He *would* bring his tools, but I wasn't about to stand out there and watch him. "Listen. Go ahead. I have to get cleaned up. Yell when you're done." I escaped into the house, undressing as I ran up the stairs.

By the time I'd changed clothes and was back outside, Spider had my bike in bits and pieces along with his thumb, which was dripping blood all over the cement drive. When he saw me, he stuck his thumb in his mouth and stood looking like a six-foot two-year-old.

"Don't move," I said, trying not to laugh. "I'll get a Band-Aid."

"I think I need a tourniquet," he mumbled.

One washcloth and two Band-Aids later, I wondered how Mrs. Jenkins had ever managed to keep Spider alive for sixteen years.

He must have known or guessed what I was thinking

because he looked down at me and kind of grinned and frowned at the same time. "I'm such a klutz. Mom says if I don't grow up she's going to put me up for adoption."

He may have been a klutz with tools but he was a *genius* at saying the wrong thing at the wrong time. I felt like saying, "Who'd adopt you?" but instead I did what I always did; I smiled. "If you grow any more there won't be any 'up' left. Maybe you should try 'down' for a change."

He took me seriously. "I tried that once in seventh grade. It didn't work."

I refrained from asking how.

"Do you know what it's like looking down on the top of people's heads?"

I sat on the bottom step. "Look at it this way. You see their best parts."

Spider, in the process of sitting down beside what was left of my bike, laughed so hard he almost knocked it over. "You say that because you're *under* standing."

I couldn't believe it! Spider was trying to be clever, and I was laughing.

We were still giggling when the *Pink Passion* rolled honking into the driveway and stopped just before it crushed both Spider and my bike.

Jav stuck her head out of one window, and Jeffrey leaned out of the other.

"What happened?"

"Have you called an ambulance?"

"Naw." Spider blushed and stood up. "I'm borrowing

45

Kim's bicycle wheel. I sprung mine on the way home from school."

"Leave the wreck and crawl in," Jav shouted as she revved all eight cylinders of the *Passion*. "We're off for Bear's. Hamburgers and fries."

"Me too?" Spider sounded as if he'd never been asked to go anyplace before by anyone, and as I climbed in the backseat, I thought that he probably hadn't.

Talking to Spider in the driveway had turned out to be easy enough, but now that we were trapped together in the backseat, I couldn't think of anything to say. I looked over at Spider. He looked as uncomfortable as I felt.

It wasn't as if we hadn't known each other all our lives, of course. I guess it was because we were in a whole new situation and weren't sure how to act. In the front seat, Jeffrey was talking to Jav, making all sorts of complicated motions with his hands. I couldn't hear what he was saying, but I could almost figure it out just by watching his hands move.

Even though he was Jav's brother and she was my best friend, I didn't know Jeffrey. By the time I met her, he was in a school somewhere in the East. Two schools, really, one directly after the other. First it was a military academy where, Jav told me, he lasted exactly one half of one semester, and then a prep school from which he actually graduated. During the summers he worked in a resort some-where out West.

The ride didn't last forever; it just seemed that way, and when we got to Bear's Den, I was the first one out of the car. A booth was empty just inside the door, and I slid in as quickly as I could. I guess I thought if I got there first it would be *my* territory and that would somehow make talking easier. Then I had to laugh at myself. I was with people I'd known or known about most of my life. What would happen if I really did meet a whole family of strangers in Sacramento?

I didn't have much time to worry. Jav and Spider folded themselves in across the table. Jeffrey sat beside me.

"You need me on this side," he said, "to make a well-balanced meal. Without me, you'd look like an anchovy with two loaves of French bread."

I looked over at him. He was gorgeous! He looked exactly like Justin Bradford in *Dreams of Young Love*: hair fine, silvery blond, eyes like mysterious black pools.

"Don't listen to him, Kim," Jav said. "He jabbers on and on and makes no sense at all. Actually, I think the parents are helping with his college education just for the pure pleasure of keeping him away from home. . . ."

After that I didn't have to worry about what to say and neither did Spider. Listening to Jav and Jeffrey talk was like watching a Wimbledon final. You never knew who was going to make the next point, but you knew they'd played each other many times before.

While Jav and Spider ordered, Jeffrey turned to me,

"You haven't had a chance to talk. You *do* talk, don't you? But being Jav's friend wouldn't give you much practice. Say something," he ordered.

"Something," I repeated, turning to place my order.

"Well," he said, and then again, "Well."

He didn't talk to me again while we ate. Instead he and Jav involved Spider in a complicated and technical discussion of bicycles in general and the Western Hills Bike Ride in grueling detail. Once, while Jeffrey and Spider were arguing gear ratios and sprockets or something, Jav leaned across the table and said, "I told Jeffrey what you're going to do. You aren't mad, are you?"

For about twelve seconds I *was* mad. It was my plan, my trip, my search, and I'd only told Jav because I needed ... that's when I stopped being angry. Maybe I'd told her because I had to use her for an excuse, but, to be more honest, because I thought she'd somehow stop me from going. It didn't matter. Jeffrey didn't really know or care about me. In fact, I decided later when the bill arrived and Jeffrey, not Jav, paid for the food, he'd forgotten that I was sitting beside him.

We went home the same way we came, Jav and Jeffrey in front, Spider and I in the back—only this time Spider talked.

He began as we pulled out of the parking lot with, "Jav's not at all stuck-up, is she?" and ended as we pulled in our driveway with, "She said she'd go bike riding with me sometime." I decided his evening had been a total success. Why wouldn't it have been? He was just like all the other kids. The only thing that made him different was how he looked, and he'd grow out of that.

Jav offered Spider a ride home, and while they were putting my bike wheel in the trunk, Jeffrey stood with me at the back door. He was just a little taller than I, maybe a couple of inches, and it was nice to look directly into someone's eyes for a change. He held on to the porch railing as if he were contemplating a balancing routine or seeing it as the basis for a handstand.

"Okay, I suppose you have to do it," he said without any kind of beginning. "And I don't imagine anyone could talk you out of it?"

"No," I answered. "No one could." I didn't bother to pretend that I didn't know what he was talking about, and I certainly didn't tell him how little it would take to make me go right over with Davey and Mrs. Mueller, monsters, dungeons, pizza, and all.

"I could try, couldn't I? Do you know how many runaway kids there are bumming around California?"

"I'm not running away."

"Why can't you stay here in Lanesport and figure things out?"

"I've tried."

"Well, let me give you some advice. Don't be out on the streets at night. Don't ask anybody anything unless it's a cop or a stewardess or somebody in authority, and always act as if you know where you're going. Get it?"

49

He sounded like Dad.

"I got it."

"I'll be aiding and abetting a minor, but I'll see you get to the airport in the morning."

"I can take the shuttle bus," I began to explain. I didn't finish because Jav was motioning for Jeffrey to get in the car.

"Seven-thirty sharp. I'll probably be imprisoned for life, but at least I'll make sure you have a proper breakfast," he whispered, and they were gone. Jav didn't even say good-bye.

Before I went to bed, I tried to call Davey. Mrs. Mueller's line was busy. I waited a few more minutes and tried again. Still busy! I gave up after three more attempts. It wasn't that I had anything to tell Davey; I just wanted to hear his voice. It's funny, but when you're away from people, the thing you miss most is the sound of their voices. No matter how hard you try to remember, you can't. Maybe voices are the first things you forget.

FOUR

Have you ever looked at yourself in the mirror after three alarm clocks have gone off? What I saw that next morning made me decide any search for my other half was definitely not worth the effort and probably it wouldn't look much different from my first half.

By seven, I was sitting by the front window, waiting for seven-thirty. Jav insisted that clocks ran slower in the morning than they did in the afternoon. I began to believe her. The streets were deserted. It was so quiet in our house that I could hear my toes wiggle in my sneakers.

I shouldn't have told Jav, and if Davey ever found out she'd told Jeffrey, I'd be disowned or dismembered. The more people who found out about my trip, the less I wanted to go. Maybe I could ride with Jeffrey to the airport and cash in my ticket. Or maybe Mom and Dad would walk in the front door and say, "Surprise! We're back." Instead the *Pink Passion* crept up the driveway.

I grabbed my backpack and eased out the front door, being sure the night lock clicked on. As I ran down the steps, Jav waved from the driver's seat. Jeffrey jumped out of the car and grabbed my backpack, and, of all people, Spider leaned out the rear window with a loud "Hi!"

"It was supposed to be a secret!" I cried.

"Crawl in," Jeffrey ordered. "You don't want to be late."

"Sure surprised you, didn't we?" Spider grinned as I settled into the backseat beside him.

Jeffrey jumped in beside Jav, and we crept slowly out the drive and into the street.

"Isn't this just like a James Bond mystery?" Jav was whispering.

"I can see the headlines now." Spider waved his hands as if he were reading. "Young girl disappears from quiet residential district."

Spider laughed. No one else did.

"There's nothing funny about disappearing girls. Or boys either." Jeffrey turned around and looked at Spider and then at me. "At least this way, Kim, we know you'll get to the airport safely. Are you sure you'll be all right after that?"

"Not if she has to use karate." Jav lurched the car onto the freeway. "Kim is probably the only person of 'Japanese extraction,' as the Heritage Club calls it, who flunked karate."

"Japanese!" Spider said, his voice almost breaking.

"Really? I didn't know you were Japanese. I just thought you were . . . well . . . kind of . . . I mean, you do look different, but that's how you've always looked."

I didn't know whether to laugh or get mad. I didn't have time to make up my mind because Jav and Jeffrey in the front seat, as if on cue, looked at each other and said, "Unbelievable!"

By now the whole mess seemed funny to me. "Just because I don't wear glasses and carry a camera around my neck. . . ."

Spider looked over at me, his face and neck growing red, "But I think it's wonderful that you're Japanese. I really do. Wonderful, too, that you're taking a trip all by yourself. Honest. It's just . . . wonderful!"

"Wonderful! Wonderful!" Jav repeated. "You got a bleep in your tape, Spider?"

I ignored Jav. I even grinned across at Spider. He blushed even redder. He'd never show up in one of my books, but for real, he wasn't so bad.

"Now, Kim,"—Jav glanced at me in the rearview mirror as she steered the car onto the airport exit—"be sure and ask for a seat in the smoking section."

"Smoking section? Does she smoke?" Spider's eyes widened.

"Of course not, but that way they'll think she's of age. Anyway, it's the safest place. The tail section."

"I think you're safest over the wings," Jeffrey argued.

"I wouldn't know." Spider looked out the window as a jet swooshed low over us. "I've never been in a plane, but I'd rather be up next to the pilot."

"Last time I was on a plane," Jeffrey went on, "we hit an air pocket and I bet we dropped two hundred feet, just like that. I just made it to the sack."

"The sack?" Spider looked puzzled.

"Spider," Jav explained, "he's talking about little bags tucked in the seat ahead of you in case you get sick."

I was beginning to get sick. I didn't want to go, but there was no chance to explain. Everyone was too busy giving me advice that ranged from Jav's "If you don't want to talk to your seatmate, just pretend you don't speak English" to Jeffrey's "If you want to read a magazine, get one before you take off. The ones on the plane are nothing but freeze-dried TV!" Spider didn't give advice; he asked questions, most of them about how many times I'd be fed on the plane.

Once we got to the airport things went so quickly that I felt as if I were a piece of furniture being shoved around. Since I had only my backpack, checking in and getting my seat assignment took just a couple of minutes, and the agent didn't even look at me when he handed me my boarding pass. Davey would have been disappointed that there wasn't a necessity for deception.

The plane was open for boarding so there was no time for the breakfast Jeffrey had promised me. It didn't seem to bother any of them, though; when I was ready to find the boarding gate, they were making plans about where *they* were going to eat.

"You'll eat on the plane." Jav guided me toward the escalator. "And be sure to keep some of your money in your bra."

Jeffrey put his arm around my shoulder and said, "You don't have to go, you know. You've got the rest of your life to find out who you are."

"But that's what I'm doing . . . starting the rest of my life."

"Have a wonderful trip, Kim." Spider was staring somewhere over the top of my head. "I mean really wonderful, and I'll get your bicycle wheel back to you as soon as I can."

Before I changed my mind, I stepped on the escalator and said, as casually as I could, "See you next week." Actually, I stole that line from Deena in *Darling Deena*, when she was leaving for an audition that would turn her into a teen-age TV star.

They were boarding mothers with little children and older people in wheelchairs when I reached the gate and found a place in a line that wound around and through the waiting section. I glanced down at my boarding pass and was adjusting my backpack when I felt a tug on my arm. I spun around, expecting the pickpocket Davey had warned me against.

It *was* Davey! And halfway down the concourse was Mrs. Mueller!

"You told!" I whispered between clenched jaws. "You fink! It was supposed to be a secret."

The line moved ahead, and I grabbed Davey's arm and tugged him along.

"I didn't tell."

"Who did? And what are you doing here?"

"I was scared. I saw this show on TV last night. Do you know what awful things can happen to kids who run away from home?"

"I'm *not* running away!"

"You didn't tell Mom and Dad, and that's running away."

"It is not." The line moved again, but I still hung on to Davey's arm. "How much does Mrs. Mueller know?"

"I'm not sure. But she found out! Maybe she guessed."

"Did you tell her everything?"

"Not quite. When she asked, I had to answer. She even asked the right questions. I made her take a vow of silence." Davey grinned. A Davey grin could melt even a Miss Sturm stare. "It's still a secret, Kim. It just got stretched out a little. And you know what?"

"What?"

"Mrs. Mueller's going to help us."

I wanted to punch him, but before I got a chance, Mrs. Mueller caught up to us and slipped an envelope into my hand. The line started moving ahead, and I didn't have time to look back.

"Call us when you get to Denver," Davey shouted as I moved through the door that led to the plane.

What was the point of secret plans when everyone knew? My trip, when I had first started planning it nearly two years ago, had seemed important and exciting. Now the magic was gone.

In spite of all the free advice for getting the safest seat on the plane, I had followed Jav's advice: an aisle seat in the back of the smoking section and "next to the stewardesses in case you need help."

I stowed my backpack, fastened my seat belt, and watched the other passengers come down the aisle, focusing blank eyes on the numbers above the seats. Cigarette sales must have collapsed, because by the time the stewardesses scurried down the aisle for the last time, I had a triple seat all to myself.

As the plane edged out of its loading slot, I looked back at the observation room. I could see a tiny silhouette in the corner of one window, frantically waving me off. I swallowed a dry lump that was filling my throat and tore open Mrs. Mueller's envelope.

I am not sure whether it was the thrust of the jet as we took off or the first line of Mrs. Mueller's note that made me gulp in a huge breath that felt as if someone had sucked all the good air out of the plane before it got to me.

As you enter the Sacramento Concourse, step five paces to the left. Stand and wave. Celia the Serene will see you along your quest. I have known Celia for years. She is completely trustworthy.

I was sixteen! I didn't need a chaperone. Maybe I could slip by without Celia spotting me, but if I knew Mrs. Mueller, she had already relayed a complete physical description of me to her friend. I read on.

Learning, remembering, forgetting. That is how we find out who we are. Mens discendo alitur.
Mueller the Mentor

It was all I needed: a dippy Dungeon Master like Mrs. Mueller managing my trip and a silly Celia waiting for me in Sacramento. How had I let myself get into such a mess?

"What's on for the weekend?" I couldn't help overhearing the stewardesses behind me as the plane zoomed up and we were airborne.

"I'm off for the week."

"In Sacramento?"

"It isn't the Swiss Alps, but there's always Lake Tahoe."

Lake Tahoe? I tried to remember my seventh-grade geography. Davey had forgotten to include a map of California. I wondered what else we'd forgotten.

"I'm on the rice run next week. Hongkong. Singapore. Tokyo."

I dug into my backpack for *A Lost Love.*

I always thought the only difference between traveling by car and traveling by plane was not miles or hours but what passed you by as you sat still. In cars, you ticked off towns and cities. In planes, it was what came down the aisle: magazines, pillows, drink cart, pick-up-drink cart, food cart, pick-up-food cart, drink cart, pick-up-drink cart, and I was in Denver.

I remembered Plan A:

—45-minute layover

—do not change planes

—report in to me

I got off the plane and found a telephone. Everybody was in a hurry except me, and if I'd known how to cash in my ticket, I would have turned around and flown back home. Home, all of a sudden, looked awfully . . . awfully . . . wonderful. Maybe I wouldn't call old Big-Mouth Davey. It would serve him right. Mrs. Mueller would probably answer anyway and insist on telling me so much stuff that I'd miss my plane.

"Excuse me. You through with that phone?" A big, blond college type with a tennis racket slung across his back looked down at me.

"I . . . I guess so. I was going to call home, but. . . ."

He smiled, then, a big-brother sort of smile. "I think you'd better, kid. I'll find another phone."

I hurriedly put through the call and stood there hoping no one would answer.

"Sybil?" Davey's voice cracked on the second syllable. Of course Davey would answer. He knew my schedule to the minute. "Are you all right?"

"Everything's going according to Plan A," I said more bravely than I was feeling. "But I wish you were along. It'd be so much more fun."

"Listen, Kim. There's been another change in Plan A."

"All right, creep. You don't have to tell me. I know. Someone called Celia. You promised it would be our secret, Davey."

"But, Kim, you can stay with Celia. It'll save us money."

"Where did Mrs. Mueller dig her up?"

"It's a long story."

"It'd better be a good one! I'll call you when I get to Sacramento. After I meet my baby-sitter."

"Believe me, Kim, Mrs. Mueller went over our Plan A and there are several holes in it. She's made a new one for us. It's called Plan Otnemarcas."

"What's that?" I asked, trying to listen to Davey and watch the loading door of my plane.

"Sacramento spelled backwards," Davey said triumphantly. "I thought of it myself."

"That figures." I groaned. "Listen, Davey. I have to go. My plane. . . ."

"Otnemarcas!" he shouted into my ear.

"Otnemarcas," I said with another groan and hung up.

. . .

60

The plane from Denver to Sacramento was no more crowded than the first flight. It was different, though, probably because I was really leaving now, from a strange airport, and the only connection to home was the sound of Davey's "Otnemarcas" ringing in my ear. Even the passengers, most of them, were different: ranchers, not cowboys but men with Stetson hats and polished boots, college kids, burned from the ski slopes, women tanned and wrinkled from the sun and hung with heavy silver-and-turquoise jewelry. I sat in the last seat and watched them file down the aisle.

An Oriental family found their place just a few seats ahead of me, a mother no larger than I, a father not much taller, and a little girl who looked like a pencil-head doll, the kind you get in grade school—a lead pencil with a tiny head where an eraser should have been, tilted eyes and straight black hair precisely cut into a frame for its face. I wondered what they were. Chinese? Korean? Vietnamese? I was like Spider. I knew they looked different, but I didn't know why. It was really weird. If I looked only at them, everyone else around looked strange, but if I looked at the other people, then the mother and father and little kid looked, not funny, but just out of place, somehow.

I didn't want to think about it, so as soon as the seatbelt sign went off, I moved to the window and stared down at the mountains. I hadn't bothered before. Iowa and Nebraska were as boring as a road map. I had never flown over the Rockies. I wondered if I could use them for Mitchell's paper: "How the Rockies Became Rocky," but it wouldn't make a very long report. Mitchell liked fat term papers. The mountains looked as if some giant mole had been moving around underneath pushing up piles of earth, and some of the taller peaks were so small at the top I felt as if I could almost reach out and pick one up like a snow cone.

"Are you Kimi Yogushi?" A stewardess leaned across the vacant seat.

I almost said no, but then I remembered who I was supposed to be.

"Did you say Yogushi?" I stalled.

"Yes. Kimi Yogushi, is it?"

I wanted to shout, "Davey. You stupe. You called Mom and Dad and they're having me bounced off the plane at Sacramento and sent back to Lanesport."

"Someone ordered a special menu for you," the stewardess went on.

"They did!"

"It's shrimp. I hope you like shrimp."

Only one person knew how much I loved shrimp. Davey! And only Mrs. Mueller would know you could order special meals ahead of flight time. They must have called the airline the night before.

I smiled up at the stewardess. "I love shrimp," I said.

My shrimp salad was delicious, especially when I noticed that everyone else had some kind of beef stew complete with technicolor carrots and little gray lumps of potatoes.

All the trays had been cleared away and I was pulling the Sacramento city map from my backpack when the Oriental woman and her little girl came down the aisle, headed for the rest room at the back of the plane. The kid wasn't very old, maybe two or three, and she sort of bounced from one side of the aisle to the other as she tried to walk, but when she got to my row, she took one look at me and climbed across the empty seats beside me with a grin so wide I thought she'd lose her teeth.

"Kimi!" she said with a giggle and held her arms out to me as if I were her long-lost sister.

"Oh, excuse me. She heard the stewardess say your name." The mother scooped the kid up and sort of half bowed. "She thinks you're her cousin," and she hurried the child into the rest room.

I slumped down in the seat. The other passengers were watching, I knew. I took a quick look around. They weren't. They were reading, sleeping, listening to piped-in music, or gazing out a window. I suppose it's always embarrassing to be taken for someone else, but at least it was halfway consoling to find out I looked like someone somebody knew. In Lanesport, I didn't look like anyone except myself.

63

I picked up *Lost in Love* and studied the cover. The girl in the drawing was about my age and she didn't look lost, she looked as if she knew exactly where she was going and why. Her hair was long and blond and curly; her eyes were seawater green, and she was wearing a swimming suit. Behind her on a beach were a lot of other people, all of them blond and smiling, too. I started reading again all over from the beginning.

Marcy stared at herself in the mirror. Oh, she hadn't changed, she knew—the same soft blond hair, the same heart-shaped face. But nothing would be the same again. How could she face the gang at the beach when her whole world had fallen apart? By now everyone must know that she'd lost out to Carla Daniels for the one remaining spot on the pom-pom squad. Her soft pink lips trembled, she felt lost.

I glanced up at the woman across the aisle who was looking at me suspiciously, I thought. So when the drink cart came by—again—I noticed that the liquor came in little bottles and you poured it yourself, and I repeated what the man ahead of me ordered: CC and Seven. The stewardess smiled and gave me the Seven without the CC. The lady across the aisle yawned and put out her cigarette.

I didn't feel like reading and there was nothing I wanted to think about, so I closed my eyes for just a minute and pretended I had blond hair and a heart-shaped face. Later, when the stewardess touched my shoulder and said "Fasten your seat belt please," I discovered I had slept my way across two states. I'd never tell Davey. He'd have it figured to the penny how much airfare I'd wasted. I looked out the window again as we started to descend. The sky could have been an ocean and our plane a huge fish circling downward into an unknown depth.

FIVE

Sybil the Seeker in Sacra Mounto! It was no longer a game. It was real. As I got off the plane, I swore that I wouldn't think about Mom and Dad or what they might say. Instead I'd forget about them until my quest was over. I didn't know if I could do it, but I was going to try. I started by acting as if landing at this particular airport were an everyday occurrence.

I didn't need a Celia the Serene, and if I didn't follow Mrs. Mueller's instructions, I could get lost in the crowd. I walked, head down, following the feet of the person in front of me until we finally turned down a small corridor where the feet disappeared through a door marked, "No Admittance. Air Personnel Only." I turned around and headed back in the direction from which we had come, I thought. Nothing looked familiar, but of course, I hadn't been looking. That was when I started getting scared. If I couldn't find my way out of an airport, what was I going to do in Sacramento? I turned around and walked in the opposite direction and finally found the gate where I'd come in. Maybe Mrs. Mueller wasn't crazy after all. I slung my backpack across one shoulder, eased over by the window and, pretending I saw someone far down the concourse, I waved.

I waited. No one came.

I watched the plane as attendants tossed luggage to waiting carts, then I turned and waved again. A young man in shorts and sport shirt came toward me. I hurriedly turned and looked the other way. What did he think I was trying to do? Pick him up? I pretended to fumble in my backpack for something important. When I looked up, he was gone.

Cautiously, I moved back to the window, waited, and waved again at the imaginary Celia the Serene, who by now I could have gladly shocked the serenity out of.

"Kimi?"

It was the young man again, running toward me.

"Kimi Yogushi?"

"Y . . . yes."

"Mom said I was to meet you here. You're not an easy person to pick up, you know."

He could have been my brother—not my Davey-brother—my other half's brother.

"You're Celia the Serene? I mean, she sent you? Celia?"

"No. I'm Ernie. Were you expecting someone else?"

"Sort of. But I guess it doesn't matter."

After all the warnings about not talking to strangers,

here I was, but since he knew my name, I figured it was all right.

"Come on, then. You have to claim your luggage down here." He started toward a stairway.

"This is all I have," I said, running after him, my backpack swinging.

He stopped and waited for me. "You travel light. Here, let me carry it."

I expected a Toyota or a Suburu, but we climbed into a VW Beetle that was losing its shell, and we took off into a swirl of traffic.

"Ever been to Sacramento before?"

"No."

"California?"

"No."

"You on vacation?"

"Yes." At least I showed him I knew two English words. I tried a complete sentence. "Does your mother always send you to pick up strange girls at airports?"

"No."

Our conversation was doomed. It wasn't like anything I'd ever read in one of my books. There, conversation sparkled and eyes met across the table in dim candlelight. Justin Bradford, the first time he met Ashley, gazed into her eyes and murmured deep feelings. Besides, Justin wasn't Japanese.

In desperation, I pointed to the field bordering the freeway. "What's growing out there?"

"Rice."

It wasn't what I had come all the way to see, but at least it required a different answer from *yes* or *no*.

"You see," he went on, "they flood these fields and fly over them in planes and drop sprouting rice seeds. The weight of the seed takes it down into the mud and by spring it grows. Beats wading up to your knees in muck."

"I bet," I agreed. "Did you ever have to do that? I mean wade around in the muck?"

He looked over at me as if measuring my IQ. "You've got to be kidding."

We lapsed back into silence after that for at least twenty rice fields.

Maybe I could write Mitchell's paper on rice fields: "Growing Rice, Now and Then." The stiff quiet must have bothered him as much as it did me because he finally dredged up another question. "You like fog?"

"Not especially. Why?"

"People who like smog go to Los Angeles. People who like fog come to Sacramento. Nobody comes here without a reason. You have family here?"

"Maybe," I said. "I don't know for sure. I think so." It sounded dumb, and I hadn't meant to tell him anything, but I couldn't just sit there saying yes and no. "My real father's Japanese. My mother's not, and my adopted dad isn't . . . and my father is dead, but maybe his family is still alive. . . ." I stopped as I was confusing myself.

69

"Hapa," he said.

"Hapa what?" I asked, expecting some kind of dumb joke.

"You're half and half. Hapa."

"Is that bad?"

He started to laugh and missed his turnoff. After he had circled a few blocks and we were on what was the right street, he looked over at me again, grinning, his teeth so white I wondered if he'd had them capped. "Hapa's fine. Everybody's got to be somebody."

"At least there's a name for me." I was finding it easier to talk after I'd seen his grin.

"We have lots of names. I'm Sansei. That's third-generation Japanese-American." He sounded proud.

"Why Japanese-American? Why not American-Japanese? I mean. . . ." I was having trouble. I had only met this Ernie—this Sansei—and I was learning things I had never thought of before. "It's hard to explain, but you see I'm not really Kimi Yogushi. I'm really Kim Andrews, but my real name is Kimi. . . ."

"You've got a lot of *reals* and *reallys* mixed up in there."

"I know."

"Don't worry about the *reallys*. You look real to me." He grinned again.

Assured, now that I knew about rice fields and Hapas and Sansei, I asked, "Your mother? She's a friend of Mrs. Mueller's?"

70

"A long-distance friend. Mom works for a magazine, and Mrs. Mueller makes up acrostics and crossword puzzles for it. Two a month. I've never met her, but Mom talks to her off and on. Brilliant old gal, Mrs. Mueller."

"Yes, indeed," I mumbled, thinking how stupid Davey and I had been thinking we could fool a Dungeon Master and a crossword maker.

"Mrs. Mueller called Mom when she heard you were coming. All I know about it is that I was supposed to meet you. Mom had a board meeting or something and couldn't get away."

We didn't talk much after that. I kept gazing out the window trying to find houses with pagoda roofs or statues of Buddha. I wondered if I'd have to take off my shoes when we got to the house. I glanced down. He was wearing Nikes.

The house would probably have paper walls and pillows to sit on or else legless bamboo chairs. Maybe we'd have to sit on the floor. I was getting hungry. I'd probably be served raw fish and green tea. His mother, with her long black hair done up like a pomegranate, would be wearing a kimono and those embroidered black slippers.

I was certainly not prepared for the woman who met us at the door of the three-car-garage, glass-and-brick house: white shorts, nautical blue top, Adidas, short hair, and a smile full of hugs. She could have been anybody's mother!

"So this is Sybil the Seeker."

Davey had told Mrs. Mueller everything!

"Or should I say Kimi?" she added as she took my arm and guided me into the house.

"Kimi," I agreed. I was getting used to the name.

"I would have met you, but this meeting. Luckily it didn't run as long as I thought. I'll bet you're famished."

"If Kimi isn't, I am," Ernie tossed my backpack on the Danish modern sofa. He didn't take off his shoes.

"We'll have a snack out on the patio, but tonight, I thought we'd try that new restaurant that's just opened. Tony's American Express. It's in a railroad Pullman car, and their specialty is T-bone steak."

Our patio snack was a fruit salad, and there were forks. I felt like a Japanese Kimi being Americanized.

The T-bones at Tony's were definitely Iowa corn-fed. I could have been back in Lanesport. When the waiter set my plate in front of me, I was so homesick, I could hardly swallow the first bite.

I had noticed, when we walked into the restaurant, that nobody paid any attention to us. At home, when Mom and Dad and Davey and I walk into a restaurant, strangers glance at Mom and Dad and Davey, but when they see me, their glances become stares.

Ernie sat across the table from me. I felt perfectly comfortable with them, which was funny since I'd just met them.

"Mrs. Mueller says you will be a senior next year," Ernie's mother said to fill up the silence.

Celia the Serene had turned out to be Mrs. Okamura. "But call me Barbara," she told me.

"Yes. I'll be a senior," I answered, "if I get through this year."

"I know what you mean," Ernie said. "The last part of high school is boring."

I liked him even better.

"I think I heard you say the same thing about your freshman year at the university," Barbara said, laughing.

"I'm not bored anymore." He winked at his mother.

"Ernie has found a cause, but let's talk about you, Kimi." She wiped the corner of her mouth with her napkin. "In one week you want to sift through forty-some years of Japanese history. Is that right?"

"I guess so."

"It's going to take some organization and fast research," she went on. "What are you really looking for? Your father's family or your Japaneseness?"

I swallowed another bite of steak. "I don't know, really, but maybe if I find one, I'll discover the other."

"Watch it, Kimi," Ernie interrupted. "You get Mother started on Japanese-American history, and you'll be here the rest of your life." He turned to his mother as if I weren't around. "Do you know what Kimi asked me on the way home from the airport? She asked why we don't say American-Japanese instead of Japanese-American."

"Obvious, Kimi. Look at our faces. We *are* Japanese. We carry the Japaneseness in our blood. We had no choice in that. We say Japanese-American because we are Japanese blood, American bred. Now, if Mrs. Mueller went to Japan and became a citizen, she would be an American-Japanese."

I tried to imagine Mrs. Mueller in such a situation. She could probably have carried it off very well.

"Before we make any plans," Barbara continued, "maybe you could explain something to me, Kimi. Is it because you're adopted that the past is so important?"

"Kimi's only half adopted," Ernie interrupted again. "Isn't that right?"

I was beginning to half like him, and I certainly liked the way he said "Kimi."

"That's the whole problem," I said. "I'm half everything: half Japanese, half adopted. I have a half brother. I'm not *all* anything." I put down my fork and leaned toward Barbara. "I know my father is dead, but he had a sister. Maybe she can add the missing part of me."

Ernie coughed and looked around the restaurant as if searching for a place to escape.

"All right, Ernie. Keep out of this," his mother said as if she were going to send him to his room without his steak.

"You've hit a nerve, Kimi," Ernie laughed. "You've got Mom up on her soapbox."

"You can tune me out then," Barbara said, resting her elbows on the table. "You see, Kimi, that's what's wrong with all of us. The missing part. You'll run into it if you find your father's people. It's the Big Whiteout. There is a chunk of years Japanese-Americans lived through and often prefer not to discuss."

"You mean the war?" I folded my napkin, feeling very adult.

"I mean the concentration camps." She spat out the words.

"But that was in Germany." At least I had learned that much in Mr. Mitchell's history class.

"Mom's talking about the Japanese relocation camps," Ernie explained, still looking around as if searching for something else to discuss.

My American history book was seven hundred pages long. There were three paragraphs about Japanese-Americans . . . one sentence about relocation camps . . . nothing about concentration camps.

"A pure euphemism, my son."

I didn't know that word, but I vowed to look it up someday if I could figure out how to spell it.

Later when the waiter came with the check, I fumbled in my jeans pocket.

"Never mind, Kimi," Barbara said, picking up the bill. "This is on Mrs. Mueller. She promised me an extra crossword puzzle next week to cover the expenses of your search."

"Mrs. Mueller?" I could have clobbered Davey for all

of his Dungeon and Dragon plans. No wonder he called Mrs. Mueller's new master plan Otnemarcas. It was Sacramento backwards, all right—everything backwards to what he and I had planned.

The telephone was ringing when we got back to the house, and Barbara rushed ahead into the den to answer it. It was then I remembered I hadn't called Davey. I was supposed to call every day as soon after six as I could, and if Mrs. Mueller answered, I was to disguise my voice and say, "Sorry, wrong number." That was before the plans were scrambled.

"Do you suppose I could call home?" I asked Barbara as she came out of the den. "I promised my little brother."

At first I thought she was going to burst out laughing; then she turned away and said, "Of course, Kimi. Go ahead. Use the phone anytime you wish."

I couldn't figure out why that seemed so funny to her, but I hurried into the den.

"Davey?" I said, trying to keep my voice from shaking when I heard his dreadful impersonation of Charlie Chan's "Ah so?"

"It's me. Kim. I'm here."

"I thought you'd never call." His voice was natural now. "Mrs. Mueller's been on the phone ever since six, and you know how long she talks. I was afraid you'd quit calling if you got the busy signal all the time. Are you all right?"

"I'm fine, Davey. And I'm starting tomorrow on the real quest."

"Uh . . . listen. Scratch Plan Otnemarcas. There's been some new developments. Go back to Plan A. I got to go now. Bye."

If I were mixed up in Lanesport, I was in complete chaos in Sacramento. Davey and his silly plans. I would do it on my own . . . and I could, too, whoever "I" was.

That night, what I thought was a sofa in the Okamura's spare bedroom, with one tug, became a mattress on the floor, and a Kimi Yogushi slept on a futon for the first time.

SIX

I woke up sometime in the night or early morning and for a moment I didn't know where I was. I wasn't frightened. I felt misplaced. What I really wanted was to be asleep, but the harder I tried, the more awake I felt and my mind kept going over all the things that had happened since I walked out of Sturm's office.

Nothing had worked out the way I thought it would. That's one thing about those books. You know everything's going to turn out all right . . . the way you know Jennifer is going to be the prom queen—that was in *Jilted Jennifer*. All you have to do is read to find out when. And everything matches. Everybody's young. Parents hardly ever goof up the story, and there are no Mrs. Muellers or Barbaras taking charge. Sometimes I think in real life the bad is planned and good things are accidental.

I started wondering if I had looked like Mom and if my real father hadn't been Japanese, would I be trying to find his family. Maybe adopted kids have to find out things that other kids never think of.

Then all the faces I'd seen started spinning around in my head—Jav's and Jeffrey's and Spider's and the little girl's on the plane. That's when I must have fallen asleep because the next thing I knew I smelled coffee and heard the faint sound of music and it was morning in Sacramento.

Barbara was sitting at the breakfast table doing a cross-word in the Sunday paper. She looked up, smiled, and gestured toward the counter. "Juice, rolls, coffee. Milk in the refrigerator. I don't talk in the morning."

I didn't mind; I was delighted. Even Davey, who usually chattered nonstop at meals, knew that breakfast was meant to be totally private. I got some milk and a roll and hid behind a section of paper. At least when I was reading, I didn't have to think.

We must have sat there for at least half an hour before Ernie came downstairs. He winked at me, put his finger to his lips, and with great exaggeration tiptoed across the kitchen.

Barbara looked at me and shook her head slowly. "So much for peace and quiet. Don't let him fool you. It's physically impossible for my son to remain speechless for more than thirty-six seconds."

Ernie ruffled her hair as he joined us at the table. "Nag, nag, nag," he said, gesturing toward his mother with his coffee cup. "The only reason she's been sitting there pretending to do the crossword is that she's been making up a hundred-item list of all the things she wants me to do today. Right, Mama?"

"Why, darling boy," she said in a fake sweet voice, "it's your vacation, remember? I wouldn't think of asking you to do anything. Of course, if you have the time. . . ."

She began with "the pool could use cleaning" and ended, just as Ernie finished his coffee, with "and the flower beds." I thought that if he did all of that, he'd never get back to his college classes.

He didn't look disturbed, though; in fact, he didn't look as if he heard her. "And while I play lawn boy, where will you be? Out on the golf course chasing that silly little white ball?"

"Of course not. We have things to accomplish—Kimi and I. Don't we?"

I nodded, but I wasn't at all sure what we were going to do. I didn't have to wait long to find out.

"First comes a short tour of Sacramento."

"Tenth Street, no doubt," Ernie said.

"Of course, my child. Not all of us have succumbed to the upwardly mobile motive." She waved a hand at the house and turned to me. "And I think you should see Kai's Fountain."

I wanted to object, but I smiled instead. I hated sight-seeing tours; I didn't want to see some stupid fountain. I hadn't practically run away from home to spend time looking at houses and parks.

"You mean," Ernie asked, "she's going to be spared the standard lecture on the entire history of the Japanese immigration to the United States?"

"Kimi has her own bit of history to attend to," Barbara said. Then she laughed. "But that topic might just come up, if she's interested."

"Oh, I'm interested in everything," I lied.

Ernie pushed back his chair. "Well, if this is going to be ethnic identity day, how about my taking you both to the Fuji for dinner? Do you like sushi, Kimi? Dad hates it, but he's not going to turn up, is he, Mom?"

I must have looked as bewildered as I felt because both of them started laughing.

"Oh, Kimi," Barbara said finally, "I'm sorry. It never occurred to me. You might have wondered." She started giggling again. "As far as I know, I still have a husband. He's in Washington for the week at some, he says, dreadfully important meeting. Now off with you, Ernie. The swimming pool is waiting, sushi or no sushi."

I didn't know what sushi was, but I didn't want to ask any more stupid questions. Instead I cleaned up the table and rinsed off the dishes while Barbara disappeared to change her clothes. The kitchen was so much like ours at home I had to keep reminding myself that I'd traveled over 1,500 miles to a city I'd never seen before.

Barbara took care of that. She was back before I could even put things in the dishwasher. "Come on, Kimi," she said. "We'll do the grand tour and then, when we get back,

81

we'll plan your week. You really don't have much time, you know."

I waited in the drive while she backed her car out of the garage. The sun was warm, more like June than April, and the fronds on the palm trees weren't even moving. At home, if the wind didn't blow, something was wrong.

Barbara's car was a little sporty convertible, and as I climbed in beside her, I thought how funny Jav would have looked in it with no room for her legs.

"Now Juppies," Barbara motioned as we drove down a broad avenue to the freeway, "live out here. Mostly professional people, mostly Sansei. Do you know the word Sansei?"

I nodded and watched the houses. They were all large with big lawns and palms and flowers everywhere. They didn't look Japanese. They just looked very expensive.

We turned onto the freeway and in a little while I could see the downtown buildings ahead of us. The skyline wasn't impressive; there weren't many tall buildings. In fact, it looked disappointingly like an overgrown Lanesport until I finally saw a roof shaped like a pagoda, shining golden in the sun.

Barbara must have guessed what I was thinking because she pulled off at the next exit and doubled back on a city street that took us past the place again.

"Chinese," she said. "They have a cultural center. Aside from a few restaurants, it's about the only Asian architecture you'll see. Even in J Town."

"What's J Town?" I asked.

"Jap town," she said. "Remember, Ernie mentioned Tenth Street? That's where most of the Japanese population is—at least those who haven't moved out south where we live."

"You call it Jap Town? That sounds so. . . ." I didn't know exactly what to say. I remembered how awful I felt when Heidi Hansen called me a Jap back in grade school.

"Sure." Barbara reached over and patted my knee. "It sounds like World War II revisited, but it's just a kind of shorthand—and a reminder, too. Don't get me started on ethnicity, at least not this morning. Look. There are the capitol and the state office buildings. Nice?"

They were. A big park, lined all around with palm trees and gardens bright and green and people walking or sitting in the sun.

"You'll want to come back here tomorrow when it's open. To the Bureau of Vital Statistics, you know, where they keep records of births and deaths and marriages. Unless you find Yogushi listed in the phone book, you'll have to do some research."

She didn't know that was the first thing I had done, looked through the phone book. There were no Yogushis.

I saw a glimmer of water shooting high into the air. "Is that Kai's Fountain?" I asked.

She did a perfect double take, and I could tell that she was trying hard to look serious, but I didn't understand why. "Nope. That comes later."

We drove around the downtown streets. They were pretty much empty and uninteresting except for one bench next to a bus stop. An old man was sitting, doing nothing, and I wished I could have asked Barbara to stop the car so I could look longer. He was very old—at least he had a wispy white beard that streamed all the way down to his lap. He wore some kind of black cap and was dressed in a long black robe that came down to his feet. I didn't know whether he was Chinese or Japanese, but he surely didn't come from Lanesport. He looked like a picture out of an encyclopedia. I wondered if that was how my grandfather looked.

"This is it," Barbara said as we drove through quiet side streets. "J Town. Most Japanese-Americans lived here before the war, and if their houses hadn't been sold, they came back after the camps. Perhaps your father grew up on one of these streets."

"Did you? Grow up here?" The houses were small but neat, brightly painted. Sometimes there was a rock garden in front, but mostly they just looked like houses.

"No. My parents lived in Los Angeles. I moved to Sacramento when I married."

"What's that?" I asked, pointing to a low brick building with a funny-looking gate.

"A Buddhist temple. Many Issei and some Nisei did not convert to Christianity in spite of the war and the pressure."

I'm not sure why I felt so surprised except that Bud-

84

dhism sounded like something out of a TV movie. I knew it existed. I'd seen pictures of statues in travelogues, but I'd never thought of real people in America being anything but Methodists or Catholics or Jews.

"Do you suppose my father was?"

"A Buddhist? When he was a child, maybe, if his parents were. Why? Don't they have temples in Iowa?"

"I don't know," I said. "Everyone I know is. . . ."

"Caucasian?" She sounded as if she were about to launch into a lecture.

I headed her off by asking another question. It was a technique that always worked with Mr. Mitchell when he called on me in history class and I hadn't read the assignment.

"You said Issei? And Nisei?"

"It's Japanese for generations. *Is*, first. *Sei*, generation. Issei. *Ni*, second. *Sei*, generation. Nisei. So it goes: Issei, Nisei, Sansei, Yansei."

"Issei, Nisei, Sansei, Yansei," I repeated. "And Hapa," I added.

"And Hapa." She looked over at me and smiled.

After showing me more of Sacramento than I ever wanted to see, she finally pulled the car to the curb. "Here's Kai's Fountain. I don't know about you, but I'm hungry."

Kai's looked small from the outside, but it was even smaller inside, and it was a fountain all right. A short counter ran along one side with three wooden booths on the other and little tables across the back. It looked odd and it smelled even stranger. I knew the soy sauce and the onions and the oil, but after that came the scent of spices that I couldn't identify.

I was so busy smelling that, until we sat down, I didn't really notice the people. The first thing I thought was that all of them were Japanese; the second thing was all of *us* were Japanese. And what they were speaking wasn't English. At least the menu printed on a slate above the counter was in a language I understood, even if I'd never heard of Oyaku Donburi, Pork Tofu, Weinie Teriyaki, or Ginger Beef. When the waitress came, she asked for our order in English.

"I'll take whatever you're having," I told Barbara. I hoped it would be a sandwich because there was no silverware on the table, just chopsticks.

"I wish I could show you a picture of your face, Kimi," Barbara said after the waitress left. "You're a walking advertisement for culture shock. Of course, I realize Kai's is a little different from most places, but haven't you ever been in a neighborhood cafe before?"

I knew she was half teasing, but I answered honestly anyway. "It's not the place. It's the people. Do they all know each other?" I thought they must because there was a steady stream of conversation that got louder as people left or came in the door.

"Mostly. They are people who live and work around

86

here. During the week it's really crowded. You see, many of them lived here before the war."

"Can you understand what they're talking about?"

If I'd really been Davey's Sybil the Seeker, I would have had the gift of understanding any langauge, even Japanese.

Barbara looked around the room. "No. I can understand a word now and then. I speak a little Japanese, but not much. Not as much as I'd like. That's something else we lost because of the war. At least I did."

I suppose I should have been glad Barbara was spending the day with me, but I wasn't too interested. All that stuff about the war was just history. I couldn't see what it had to do with me, but to be polite, I said, "It's like being in two places at the same time. Outside it's just everyday America, but in here it's like a foreign country. I can't understand anyone, and I don't even know how to use chopsticks."

Barbara laughed. "Learning to use chopsticks is a lot easier than learning Japanese, believe me. But how can your own people, and they *are* you know, seem so strange to you?"

So I told her all about my family and what I knew and didn't know about my father, and about what it was like growing up in Lanesport. By the time I got to Inez Sturm, the waitress was back with bowls of something and what looked like little jars of pickled cabbage.

"She'll need a fork and spoon," Barbara said. The waitress looked surprised, but she didn't say anything, just nodded.

We didn't talk much after that. I was too busy concentrating on all the new tastes. It wasn't at all like the one Chinese restaurant in Lanesport that sent out sweet and sour pork in soggy little cardboard containers. I kind of envied Barbara's skill with the chopsticks. I thought the food must taste better that way. I knew I should be thinking about what I was going to do the next day and about the questions Barbara might be able to answer, but somehow for once the "now" was enough.

Barbara let me pay my share of the bill, but she wouldn't let me pay hers. As we left, she asked, "Do you mind if we stop for a minute? There's a Japanese grocery store around the corner and I need a few things that the supermarkets don't carry."

I hadn't come to Sacramento to visit a grocery store. I wanted to find my family.

We walked down the empty street, around a corner, past a playground to the store. It, too, was small and crowded, with shelves full of things I'd never seen before—bags of rice as large as bed pillows, strange-looking vegetables, mysterious cellophane-wrapped food that I couldn't identify, and everywhere the labels were in Japanese. I suppose it was silly, but it had never occurred to me that everything in America wasn't written in English.

Barbara was finished with her shopping long before I

was ready to stop exploring, but she was patient and walked around with me, explaining some of the things and telling me what they were used for and how they tasted. It really was a guided tour.

As we drove back to the freeway through the streets, Barbara pointed to a sprawling brick building. "That's Ernie's school."

It wasn't like any college I'd ever seen, much too small and quite shabby. I said so.

"No, it's not Berkeley," Barbara said. "That's where he goes to college. But this is his *school*. My frivolous, only son has found a cause." She was smiling, and she sounded pleased.

"What cause?" I asked. I couldn't quite imagine Ernie's being too serious about anything—certainly not about some old school building.

"It's called the West Side Opportunity School. It's for Asian immigrants. Boat people, survivors of Vietnam, newly arrived Chinese, Japanese, for anyone who needs help learning the language, getting adjusted, finding training for jobs that didn't exist where they came from."

"Does he teach there? How can he do that and go to college at the same time?"

"No, he's not a teacher, but he may be someday. Right now he's a volunteer. Whenever he's home he does whatever they need. Sometimes he's a janitor, sometimes he helps in the kitchen at lunchtime, sometimes he tutors people. He jokes about it and says it keeps him out of trouble, but it's changed him in many ways. All of them good."

We drove past the capitol again. "Ernie was a lot like you," she said and then looked startled at her own words. "I didn't mean that badly."

It sounded bad to me, the way she'd said it, as if I were a little kid being scolded for something that wasn't my fault. She must have sensed how I felt.

"I just meant that for a long time, while Ernie was growing up, he had no more sense of what it means to be Japanese-American than you do. For you, there's a reason —lots of reasons. From everything you've told me, you are alone. Oh, I don't mean you don't have a whole family who loves you, but you have no friends with the same ethnic background. No past to learn from."

"But Ernie did, you mean? And he didn't learn?"

"Not just Ernie, but a whole generation. My generation, too. It goes back to the camps. Maybe because our parents or grandparents wouldn't talk about such an important part of the past. Maybe for us something was left out. It's hard to explain, but so many of us grew up without an identity. You see it in the larger cities especially. We were chameleons. Because we didn't have the special Japanese sense of ourselves, we took on the attitudes, the habits, even the language of others. It didn't matter which group —Black, Chicano, Puerto Ricans—any people who maintained a sense of who they were. But that's a speech I promised Ernie I wouldn't make. At least not this early in the afternoon." I was glad when she stopped talking and we pulled into the driveway at her house.

"No more lectures," Barbara promised. "Look. It's a beautiful warm afternoon. Did you bring a swimsuit with you?"

I shook my head. When I left Iowa I hadn't been thinking about swimming pools.

"You can borrow one of mine, if you like. We're about the same size. And you can run away from me for a while and sit in the sun or swim or sleep, or whatever. And I promise, no more history until you ask."

"Thank you," I said, and I really meant it. "It's just that there are so many things to sort out, to put together." And then I lied, but just a little. "It wasn't really a lecture anyway."

As she handed me the swimsuit, I asked something that had been bothering me ever since I had arrived. "You don't even know me. Why are you being so nice to me? I understand about Mrs. Mueller, but. . . ."

Barbara didn't answer right away; then she laughed. "Don't tell me you want the rest of my lecture? Kimi, I'll put it in one sentence. You could be my sister . . . or my daughter . . . or me. Isn't that enough?"

It was enough.

It was quiet by the pool. The only sound came from a radio in someone's backyard or the occasional sound of a jet plane high above. I thought about what Barbara had said about "Japaneseness." It sounded so much more human than "ethnic awareness," which had been a two-day unit in Mr. Mitchell's history class. Maybe I had the whole thing backwards. When I thought of myself as Japanese, I was really thinking of the outside me—of how I looked different from the other kids. On the inside, I didn't feel Japanese at all, and I was pretty sure that Barbara did. Ernie, too.

Then I started wondering about Jav and Spider and, of all people, Heidi Hansen. What was she like on the inside? How did she feel? Did her inside and outside match any better than mine? I'd ask her, maybe, sometime when I got back to Lanesport. And of course I'd go home even if I did find my father's family. I could see them now, begging me to stay and finish my senior year in California and go to the university and major in, maybe, Japanese art. And who was to know but what someone might decide to remake a mini-series of *Shōgun* and I might try out for a bit part. Or was that Chinese?

The afternoon slid toward evening, and the only time I saw Barbara was when she brought me a glass of iced tea and then disappeared into the house again. I asked her if she didn't like lying in the sun, and she said, "We are women of color, but I don't like the color I'd turn—yellow."

That was something else I always felt funny about—the color of my skin. I didn't like to think about it, and I certainly couldn't joke about it. Besides, I wasn't yellow and neither was Barbara. Peach, maybe, not yellow like a lemon.

Sometime late in the afternoon, Ernie wandered out to the patio. "Been in the water yet?" he asked.

"It's too nice right here. Besides, I ate so much for lunch, I'd probably sink straight to the bottom."

"Come on," he said. "You need some exercise. If I'm taking you and Mom to dinner, you have to be hungry. Besides, I spent half the morning cleaning the pool and that's a waste of time if no one uses it." He walked to the edge, did a perfect racing dive, and slid under water half the length of the pool. He swam beautifully, with sure, powerful strokes that cut through the water, yet barely disturbed the surface.

He *was* handsome! Not like a character in a book, but handsome in a different way—black hair, black eyes, a body the color of toast that's done just right. Would he look the same way to me back at the municipal swimming pool in Lanesport with all the kids from school? How would they have seen him . . . and me? I tried to imagine us in a story like *Love for Lonnie*, but I'd never met anyone like us in those books.

That evening, sitting in still another restaurant, it occurred to me that so far my search for family had definitely centered around history and food. I'd flown all the way to Sacramento to find out about my father, and what I'd learned was how to handle chopsticks—not very well, but with Ernie's and Barbara's help, I could at least get food from bowl to mouth.

"Even a Hapa should have table literacy," Ernie teased.

"Besides, it's not so hard. See, we cheat by holding the rice bowl close to our mouths, so if we make a slip and drop something, no one notices. Right, Mom?"

"That," Barbara said, "is a bad example of ethnic humor. But for once my son is right. How do you like the sushi, Kimi?"

I didn't like it. I loved it! I wasn't sure whether it was because of the way it looked, like little jeweled cubes in a box or because of the tastes—sweetish sometimes, spicy sometimes—all the flavors and textures. For the first time I realized that food melting in the mouth was not a cliché.

I was content to sit and eat and listen to Ernie and Barbara tease each other and talk about plans for the week. I wondered what Mr. Okamura was like and if he would have approved of me, a stranger, appearing out of nowhere and staying with his family. I tried hard *not* to think of what Mom and Dad would say.

Before we left that evening, Barbara suggested how I should spend the next day. "No Yogushis in the phone book," she began. "But that's not surprising. The grandparents might well be dead and the daughter would probably have married. I think you'll have to start your search before the war—before the camps. You may not find your answer, but at least you'll have some questions."

I already had a question—why had I ever come to Sacramento?

SEVEN

"The Bureau of Vital Statistics first," Barbara instructed as she dropped me off at the capitol grounds the next morning. "It's on the third floor, I think, but you'd better check."

Vital Statistics. It sounded like a new breakfast cereal, but that was why I was in Sacramento—to find my vital statistics.

The department looked like a bank with tellers at little cages and lines of people waiting at each window.

"Is everybody looking for somebody?" I asked the lady ahead of me as I took my place in what I thought was the shortest line. From the back she looked like the motherly type—broad shoulders and cushiony arms—a stranger even Jeffrey would approve of my speaking to.

"Everybody's tracing their genealogy. It's the latest kick." Her hands were full of papers. "Isn't that what you're here for?"

"Sort of. I'm trying to find my father."

The woman turned around and looked at me the way Mom does when I split an infinitive. "You mean you've lost him? Did he say he was coming in here?"

"No. No, I mean, I'm supposed to get a copy of his birth certificate."

"Oh." She turned and looked at me again. "Did you fill out that form over there? On the table. It'll cost you three bucks. Didn't he tell you?"

"No . . . He's. . . ." I had forgotten all the answers I'd rehearsed so carefully.

"Not trying to discourage you, kid, but you know records got sort of screwed up out here during the war. Japanese, I mean."

"I know," I said as I headed for the table. I found the proper form and carefully printed my father's name: Kenji Yogushi. Seeing it there in so many letters made him seem more real already.

Someone had taken my place in line, so I moved on down to another. Davey figured up once that he spent one whole month out of every year of his life waiting in line: hot lunch, grocery, ticket, rest room. Davey exaggerates, but by the time I got up to a window for my turn, I was ready to agree with him.

A tall lady with blue eyes that looked but didn't see glanced at my form and sighed. "You an American citizen?"

"Oh, yes. Of course." I had never been asked that before.

"This your father?"

96

"Yes, ma'am." I smiled my best smile.

"He an American citizen?"

"Yes." I smiled again.

"Reason," she read. "To learn grandparents' name and address."

"Yes." I was getting tired smiling.

"You mean. . . ."

She sounded like Miss Sturm. In fact, she was beginning to look like Miss Sturm.

"The correct spelling," I lied. "I'm tracing my family's genealogy—for school. It's an assignment. And I don't spell very well in Japanese. Besides I need the address where they lived." I smiled so sweetly I almost gagged.

"One minute, please." She sighed again, an even bigger sigh, as if she had been saving all her breath for this final one, and disappeared behind a bank of files. Evidently, computers had not come to Vital Statistics.

I waited and waited and waited and all the people lined up behind me sighed and shuffled and grumbled and waited, too. What if my father wasn't born here? Just because he'd lived here didn't mean he was born here. Maybe the whole idea was crazy anyway—coming clear out to Sacramento to look for a family that probably didn't exist anymore. I was about ready to think the clerk had passed out on her last sigh, when she returned, handed me a photostatic copy, took my money without a single sigh, and called out, "Next?"

I escaped to the hall, found a bench, and sat down. I

felt as if I had just finished ten laps around the Lanesport gym. I was afraid to look at what I'd found. Finally I glanced down and read for the first time my grandmother's name: Noriko Kurihara Yogushi, mother, aged 19.

I couldn't believe it. She was only three years older than I when she had my father. Then I saw my grandfather's name: Yoki Yogushi, aged 35.

Names don't make a family, I know, but somehow I felt as if that other half of me actually belonged to someone, even if the names did look strange. Then I saw the address. Barbara and I had probably driven by the very place the day before. They had existed, my own family, and the address proved it.

"You find your father?"

"Yes." I slid over and the motherly woman I had talked to sat down and slipped off her shoes.

"Hard on the old grape stompers, this genealogy stuff."

"I'll say. And they ask so many questions."

"I heard you say you were trying to find an address. You know, up on sixth floor they have all the old telephone directories of the city from way back. You might want to double-check up there. But on the other hand, maybe your grandparents wouldn't have spoken English, so I guess they wouldn't have needed a phone, would they?"

"Maybe not . . . but I can look." I wanted to thank her for helping me, but I didn't want to tell her everything.

"Funny, aren't we? We have to know where we come from when the important thing is where we're going."

"I guess so," I agreed. "What did you find?"

Jav always said when you didn't want to talk about something, you asked questions of the other person.

"Didn't find what I wanted. Got what I found. Discovered my great-grandfather was not upper crust Bisignano. Would you believe lower crust?"

Bisignano. It could have been an Italian sports car.

"Does that mean you have to start over?" Sometimes it's hard to think up enough questions to hide behind.

"Yep. It means I got to get stomping now. I'll be back this afternoon and start through the telephone books again." She wriggled her feet into her shoes, tucked papers into a purse, and stood up. "Well, see you around, kid. All you have to do in this business is keep asking questions."

"Good-bye, and thank you," I called after her.

I was on my own at last. I considered going up to the sixth floor and looking through telephone books, but that didn't sound half as exciting as the address. I didn't want to reconsider. I ran out of the building, my sneakers slapping on the stone floor, down the shaded walk to the street, and hailed a taxi.

"Four-sixteen Tenth Street," I said, as I settled back in the seat. We slithered through traffic and I began to lose my sudden burst of courage. What could I expect to find at an address that was at least forty years old? And what was

99

I going to do if I did find something . . . or somebody? I told the cab driver to let me out at the corner of Tenth Street. I waited until he drove away; then I walked slowly down the street searching for the house number. An older couple passed me, nodded and smiled. I smiled back. A mother pushing a toddler in a stroller nodded and smiled, too. I smiled back. Then an awful thought hit me. I was in what Barbara called Jap Town. Everyone assumed I belonged. It was Lanesport in reverse.

The house looked like any other house—story-and-a-half bungalow, open porch, white pillars. I knew exactly how the inside looked: two bedrooms and bath on one side, living room, dining room, kitchen, back porch on the other. Front yard, backyard, garage. Someone had come out the front door and was sitting on the porch, so I hurried by and circled the block and strolled by again.

"You lost or just gawking?"

Her gray hair, thick, not wispy, and neatly bound into a bun and her eyes, as round as a cat's, were all I could see of her over the porch railing.

"I was just looking at your house." I took a couple of steps toward her.

"Not another one!"

I stopped. "I don't think so. I don't know what you mean. I. . . ."

"You're all the same. You're going to tell me your great-grandfather lived here before the war, buried the family savings before they carted him off to Jap camp, and could you dig up my backyard and see. The answer is no. I've owned this house for years and no one has a right to come in and inspect my property."

Dad always said cranky people were like Brazil nuts. You had to crack their shells to get to the meat. I wasn't too sure this one could be cracked, but I was going to try.

"Yes, ma'am. But you see I'm an orphan from back East. Kim Andrews. I've saved my money to come out here to see if I could find my family." I edged toward the front steps. "All through school I baby-sat, waited tables, and cleaned houses. I was raised in a foster home and I have to go back on the bus tonight, and all I have is this address. They said it was on my blanket when they found me on the doorstep of the orphanage."

She hadn't yelled at me again, and she looked as if she was believing me. It was a lousy story, but it had been used in *A Mother for Marcy*.

"How'd you get here?"

"Walked from the bus station. Do you mind if I sit down? It won't bother you, will it? I won't stay long, but I rode all last night on the bus and I'm sort of tired."

Davey would have been proud of me. Mrs. Mueller would have made me a Dungeon Master. Dad would have grounded me for a week.

"I don't mind. Sit down. You do look a bit peaked."

"Thank you," I answered with a fake sigh. "You're very kind."

"Want a drink of water? It's all I got."

"If it wouldn't be too much to ask." I sat down on the bottom steps and wiped my forehead with the back of my arm.

The water was cold, and she had added two ice cubes. I really was thirsty.

"Don't think I can help," she said as she settled back into her rocker. "But I suppose I can tell you what I know."

Her hands were all knuckles and her legs lumpy beneath white elastic stockings. I was beginning to feel guilty about the big story I'd made up, but Miss Turner told us once in English class that fiction was the lie made truth. I decided to go along with fiction.

"My father bought this house in . . . what was it? Forty-two. Forty-three, maybe," she began without my prompting her with another question. "Bought it when they cleared the Japs out of here and carted them out to the prison camps at Tule Lake. I guess you'd have to admit he struck a pretty good bargain. Didn't have to pay too much for it, but you can see why. If you put every house here on Tenth Street up for sale at the same time, you know they're going to go cheap."

"I know." I didn't know, but I didn't want her to stop. Jav says the other way to keep a conversation going is to insert "I see" or "I know" or "Is that so?"

"When Pa died, I got the house, moved back here after my kids were grown and my husband gone."

"Did you ever see the people . . . the people who sold the house?"

"No. We were living in the valley then. Three kids, me the oldest. Pa came home and said he had a house in town for us and we moved in."

"Did you ever hear the name of the man who sold it?"

"Never paid any attention. All I can say is, he was Japanese. I was young back then. Got a job in a defense plant. We were busy winning a war with the Japs, not learning their names."

I rubbed my hand across the step. My family had walked down these very steps. My own father even, and now I was here. I stood up and looked at the house again, trying to imagine my family sitting on the porch with my father racing down the walk and around to the backyard to play with his sister. I didn't want to go inside the house. The outside was enough.

I couldn't think of any more questions, and she didn't look as if she wanted me to stay any longer, so I said, "I must get back. I don't want to miss my bus. Thanks so much for letting me talk to you."

"No bother." She rocked back in her chair. "Have a nice trip back. If I was you, I wouldn't go digging up the past. People can't help what they did."

"I guess not," I agreed and walked away. She was a Brazil nut, all right, but Dad was right. You had to crack the shell.

I hurried down the street. I didn't dare take a taxi after that wild story I'd told her. I had studied the city map of Sacramento, so I knew my way around even if I'd never actually spent any time in the place. I turned right off Tenth Street and wondered if I should have turned left. Davey says you always tend to turn to the right because the earth rotates that way. I finally decided I'd made the correct turn when the numbers on the streets started going down from ten.

I had just passed Seventh Street when I drew in my breath and stopped dead still right in the middle of the sidewalk. The woman had said her father bought the house when "they cleared out the Japs and sent them off to prison camps at Tule Lake." My father . . . my grandmother . . . my grandfather . . . were they the "thems" who were sent off to prison? My history book hadn't called them prison camps. Neither had Mr. Mitchell's World War II films. The woman had said Tule Lake. I'd never heard of it. It sounded like a vacation spot, but it wasn't. It was one of those relocation camps Ernie had mentioned and that Barbara called concentration camps.

I started walking again, slowly at first, on the edge of the sidewalk; then, as if my feet were doing the thinking, I walked faster and faster until I was almost running.

Miss Turner, our English teacher back in Lanesport, told us once that people walk in iambic pentameter rhythm —that's five beats of short-long. Then she'd march around the classroom, half singing, beating out:

The *cur*-few *tolls* the *knell* of *part*-ing *day*
The *low*-ing *herd* winds *slow*-ly *o'er* the *lee.*

But my feet were pounding out different words to iambic pentameter:

They *put* my *fa-*ther *in* a *pris-*on *camp!*

Was that why Mom never wanted to talk about my real father! He'd been in prison!

The Bisignano lady at the Bureau of Vital Statistics had said to try old telephone directories. I could find out when my family came back from the camps. I ran the rest of the way back to the same building. After about ten inquiries, I found the directories among stacks of shelves filled with old city records and musty-smelling legal papers.

"Took my advice, did you?" The lower-crust Bisignano peeked around the end of one shelf. "Are you finding what you're looking for?"

"Not really." I tried not to sound the way I was feeling.

"Listen, kid. Maybe I can help. I don't want to be nosy, but what *is* it you're after?" She leaned up against the shelf.

At first I was going to tell her the same story I'd told earlier, but something about the way she squished her eyes together and looked out at me from little slits made me decide to tell the truth for a change. Jav says when all else fails, tell the truth . . . and run.

"I want to find my father's family. I never knew him. He died before I was born."

"What have you found so far?" She moved over beside me.

"Names and an old address."

"Okay, then. Start here in this nineteen-forty-one directory. Keep looking through forty-two, forty-three . . . the name will probably drop out then, but keep going up through . . . oh, say, fifty-two or fifty-three. You realize, of course, they rounded your people up after Pearl Harbor —out here—and sent them off to camps in California, Colorado, wherever. They did the same thing in Canada, but you probably know all about that."

I didn't know all about that, but I was learning.

"If your family lived here in Sacramento, they probably ended up at Tule."

I vowed I'd get a map and look up Tule Lake.

"I'll leave you alone now. If you need any more help, holler."

"I will, and thanks." I pulled out the directory and thumbed through to the Y's.

There it was! Yogushi, Yoki, 410 Tenth Street. I reached for the nineteen-forty-two directory. There it was again: Yogushi, Yoki, 410 Tenth Street.

Maybe they hadn't been imprisoned. I reached for the next book. No Yogushi. I kept going, the directories piling up beside me. '44, '45, '46, '47, '48, '49. No Yogushis.

"How's it going?" The Bisignano face appeared around the corner of the stacks again.

"I found them. But I lost them."

"Maybe they didn't come back here. Some of them went back to Japan."

106

"They did?" I shut 1949. "I give up. It's not worth a trip to Japan, that's for sure."

"Keep going." She pulled out five more volumes. "Go up to at least 1959. You never know."

I kept going—'50, '51, '52.

"Here they are!" I shouted. Bisignano reappeared.

"Same address?"

"No. Different one."

"Copy it down, and let's look to see if they appear the next year." She thumbed through the next volume.

"What do you know. They aren't here."

"Are you sure?" I looked over her shoulder. "What do you suppose happened?"

"I don't know. A lot of things could have. This Yoki your grandfather?"

"Yes."

"He may have died. Lot of them came out of the camps in poor health, particularly the men. Business gone, money gone, spirit, too. Why don't you keep looking through— maybe ten years more? If you can't find anything, at least you have an address. In this business you grab at any clue to keep going. It's a game, really."

"Sure," I mumbled.

"I've got to go, but you keep looking. If you need to find them bad enough, you'll find them."

There were no more Yogushis. I put the books back on the shelf. I had wasted a whole day, and all I had was another address, an address twice as old as I.

Outside the late afternoon air was fresh, and I sat on a park bench and breathed in. History was depressing. It was there and you couldn't change it. Of course, if I didn't think about it, it didn't exist. The past was only in books and in my mind, and it existed only when I read about it or thought about it. I decided to quit thinking.

I checked to see if I had enough money to take a taxi. When I crawled into the cab, I changed my mind about going back to Barbara's. Sometimes I surprise even myself.

"West Side Opportunity School, please."

I'd see if I could catch a ride back with Ernie. I'd tell him about the names I'd found on the birth certificate and the address on Tenth Street, but as for the other address, I'd keep that to myself. I wasn't sure I wanted to carry my quest any further.

I spotted Ernie's car in the parking lot, paid the cab driver, and sat down on the lawn to wait. Sacramento was beautiful. They were probably still having sleet and snow back in Iowa. I wondered what Jav was doing . . . and Jeffrey . . . even Spider. Davey I didn't have to wonder about. He was either devising more quests for Mrs. Mueller or else he was kicking a soccer ball around. He claimed soccer was the only game, besides pool, that could be played scientifically.

Then I started thinking about Mom and Dad in Chicago, even though I didn't want to. Dad was probably attending meetings and Mom was shopping and going to all the plays she could squeeze in. And then I wanted to go home in the worst way. I remembered, when they left that morning, how Dad had said, as he always did, "Hug or a handshake?" Why had I chosen a handshake? Mom didn't really say anything. She just cradled my face in her hands and whispered, "Kimi." She didn't often call me Kimi. Did she understand more than I thought? The whole trip was wrong. Why did something seem so right when you planned it and so wrong when you did it? Why couldn't I be satisfied the way I was? I was a not-very-tall Kim Andrews with sort of funny eyes, sort of different-colored skin, and sort of odd-looking straight black hair. So what? I'd forget about that second address I'd found and tell Barbara I was going home, if not tomorrow, then at least the next day.

And why hadn't Mom told me about my father's being in a prison camp? Was that one of his silences? I looked up at the sky. It amazed me that someone way back in Lanesport could look up and see the same sky . . . the same sun. Maybe it hurt Mom to look back on a time that was sad for her. I guess mothers hurt sometimes, too. I'd never really thought about that, but I bet they must.

The West Side Opportunity School didn't look much like an opportunity, more like some kind of factory. The playground swings were gone, and all that was left was a black-topped parking lot with Ernie's car and a couple of pick-up trucks. The building was old, old enough to have been there when my father was little. Maybe he'd even gone to school here.

Finally, Ernie and a woman came out of the building.

"Kimi! What are you doing here?"

"Thought I'd catch a ride home with you."

"Sure. I just offered to drop Mrs. Enomoto off at her house." And then to the woman, "This is the Kimi I was telling you about."

She was older than I had thought from a distance; in fact, she was even older than my mother. She had little wings of white in her black hair and lines at the corners of her eyes.

"How do you do, Kimi." I didn't have to be told she was a teacher.

"Get in." Ernie motioned toward the car. "And tell us what you found out today."

"Not much," I said as I climbed into the backseat, thinking there are times when it pays to be five foot one—when you have to sit in the backseat of a compact car. "Found an address on my father's birth certificate."

"Did you follow up on it?" Ernie asked.

"Took a taxi out there," I said and told them about the woman on the porch.

"I'm sure her father got the house for a very good price," Mrs. Enomoto said with an edge to her voice. "What are you going to do next?"

"I haven't decided."

"Listen." Ernie half turned to look back at me. "How about forgetting about the big search. A bunch of us are having a party tonight. Do you want to come along?"

"I think that would be lovely for Kimi," Mrs. Enomoto

chimed in, and I had a funny feeling the two of them had talked it over before they even saw me.

"I didn't bring any clothes . . . not anything special." I hurriedly tried to remember what I had packed.

"It's no dress-up thing," Ernie said. "And you'll meet some interesting people."

After we'd dropped Mrs. Enomoto at her house, I hoped that Ernie wouldn't ask any more questions. I needn't have worried because he began talking about things that had happened at school that day and didn't finish until we pulled into the driveway.

"I think I'll go for a walk," I said as we got out of the car. "Is that all right? I won't be gone long, but I feel like walking."

"Sure," he said. "No problem. Mom won't be home for another hour at least. See you later."

The last thing in the world I felt like doing was walking. I figured I must have covered half of Sacramento in the last six hours, but I wanted to call Davey, and I knew there was a shopping center not too many blocks away. I could have called from the house, I suppose, but I wanted to be alone.

I got Davey on the first ring even though it wasn't quite six. He must have been waiting by the phone. "Are you alone? Can you talk?"

"I am alone. I can talk." He was sounding like an agent for the CIA.

"Listen, Davey. I don't know what to do. I've got an

address. Found it in an old telephone directory. But I can't just go up and knock on the door without some excuse. I can't just say, 'Hello. Are you a Yogushi? I'm a Yogushi, too,' because I don't think they know I even exist."

"You could pretend you were delivering pizzas and you got the wrong address."

"Davey! You can do better than that! Or do you think I should just quit and come home? I don't know. I guess I don't really care anymore about finding out things."

"You can't quit!" he practically shouted. "It'll spoil everything."

"Well, what should I do? Really. I'm serious. I want to come home. I really do."

"You can't quit in the middle of the game. It's against the rules."

"I can quit if I want to."

"No, you can't."

Davey's problem was he couldn't tell fact from fantasy.

"Why can't I?"

"Because I'm the Dungeon Master. I *make* the rules. All I need is some more time. I'll figure out a plan. Can you call me tomorrow?"

"When? How about six? Why don't you go over to our house and I'll call you there?"

"I can't!"

"Why can't you?"

"Mrs. Mueller would think something was wrong. I'll be waiting here."

"Okay. But you better have a good plan or a good reason or I'm coming home."

"I will"

When I got back to the house, Barbara was busy filling a briefcase with papers. "Meeting again," she explained. "Ernie said you hit a dead end today."

"Yeah. As far as the Yogushis were concerned everything sort of stopped when the war began."

"Not just for the Yogushis. For all of us," Barbara said. "Why don't you take the day off tomorrow and look through some of the books in the study? They'll give you a start on the stopping." She closed the briefcase. "And maybe tomorrow, we'll have a chance to talk."

I thanked her just as if I hadn't decided that I didn't want to know anything more about Japanese-Americans or relocation camps or about that long-ago war.

Ernie had said it wasn't a dress-up party, and it was a good thing. My backpack hadn't allowed room for party clothes. I dumped everything I owned on the floor and pulled out a clean pair of jeans. I was putting them on, balancing on one leg, when I stopped. This was a date! My first date ... with a boy. Not a boy, a college man! I could hardly wait to tell Jav. Maybe Ernie didn't see it as a date, but it was. It had to be. He'd asked me!

I tore off the jeans and headed for the shower. If I couldn't be dressed up, I could at least be clean ... and maybe even alluring. Scents had the power to attract. I had learned that in biology. There was only one major problem. Ernie seemed a lot more like a brother than a boyfriend, but I didn't have to tell Jav that part of it.

I was hurrying down the stairs when I heard Barbara talking on the phone in the den: "Oh, I think so. I'll let her do her own thing, don't you think? Encourage, but not be nosy."

I stopped on the stairs and listened. Jav says there are times when one must forget all social graces.

"Oh, I'll keep an eye on her, don't worry. Why don't you get in touch with me tomorrow . . . at my office?"

She was talking about me, I knew. And she must have been reporting in to Mrs. Mueller. I was being checked on. Spied on. I hurried out the front door.

"I'm not too crazy about parties," I said as I climbed in beside Ernie, trying to talk naturally.

"Don't worry," he said. "It's just a bunch of people."

"Are you sure it's okay? I won't know anyone and no one will know me."

"They're just people from around here. Some of them I grew up with. Some I met in college. They talk a lot, but they won't bite."

Cars lined the street in front of the small brick house that sat half hidden by shrubbery and palm trees.

I didn't have a chance to be nervous because, once we were through the front door, I was too busy trying to sort out people and remember names to think about myself or how I looked. It was nothing like the high school parties back in Lanesport. For one thing, I had a date and besides, at home, even kids who'd been with each other all day in school acted uncomfortable at a party with big, awkward lumps of silence, but here people were all talking—talking to each other, not about each other either, but about books and ideas and theories. Anyway, at home all the kids were white, except for me. Here everybody was a different color. If you live in Lanesport, you start believing there's only one color in the world. Here we were every shade you could imagine—from Minnie, a big woman with skin so black it almost glowed, to me.

When Minnie saw Ernie, she put her arms around him in a smothering hug.

"As you can see, she likes me," Ernie said laughing, "but you can imagine what she could do to you if she didn't."

Minnie looked down at me. She was as tall as Jav and must have weighed three times as much, but she wasn't fat, just plain big. "And where did you find this beautiful girl?"

No one had *ever* called me beautiful.

"This is Kimi. She is visiting us from Iowa."

"How nice!" Minnie said. "And you look like you could use a hug, too."

It was the kind of hug that made me feel instantly homesick.

"And if this boy," she turned to Ernie, "would give up rice and start eating right, he might amount to something."

"Can't you see me eating collard greens with chopsticks?" Ernie patted her arm. "I'd starve. Minnie, look after Kimi for a minute, will you? I'll get us something to drink." He started weaving his way through the crowd.

"Well, honey," Minnie turned toward me. "Who'd you like to meet? There's some good people here. Would you like to meet Mr. Graham? He's the guest of honor."

"Who's he?" I hadn't realized it was a party for someone.

Minnie looked down at me blankly. "You don't know who Lorenz Graham is? Don't kids read books in Iowa?"

"Of course." I didn't offer any specifics.

"Graham's a writer. A well-known writer. He did a whole string of books for young readers: *South Town, North Town*, and he's one fine gentleman. See, that's him in the chair over there."

She took my arm and, like a tugboat behind a luxury liner, I followed her across the room.

I didn't know what a writer was supposed to look like, and I never imagined one could be alive in the same room with me. I never thought of a writer being Black, either. He was a small, gray-haired man, dressed in a dark suit that made him look like a preacher or a college professor. A whole bunch of people hovered around him, asking questions and listening to his answers as if there was going to be a test the next day.

"And here is a reader," he said when Minnie introduced me. "I can always tell."

"You can?" I said, hoping he wouldn't ask me if I had read any of his books.

116

"Always," he repeated. "Readers look curious. They want to know the answers to questions they haven't even thought of."

I smiled as if I'd read every word he'd written. Minnie didn't smile. She just looked down at me and sort of muttered under her breath, "Well, do tell!"

I ended up in a corner with a small group—someone from a Dakota reservation, a Mexican student from some university, a young man who insisted he was Asiamerican, and a girl who looked sort of like me and who, when I asked if she were Japanese, too, said no she was Laotian.

"Behavior conforms to stereotypic language," she said. I thought she was talking to me.

"You're wrong," someone argued. "Behavior shapes stereotypes. Ethnicity is a learned code. Approach the problem on a fully algorithmic form."

"Impossible," someone else shouted. "Asian-Americans are at the interface of two cultural systems and look for courses of action that will accommodate their traditional values in the roles thrust upon them."

"The educational system is at fault!" someone standing behind my chair announced. "It codifies self-perceptions by linguistic labels with its unilineal and monocultural approach."

I thought they were speaking English, but I wasn't sure. I quit listening then and started looking around at people's shoes. You can tell a lot from people's shoes. If they're wearing clunky shoes, they tuck them back under their chairs. If they're wearing fancy shoes, they cross their legs out in front.

"We are carriers of our own cultural heritage and WASPs. . . ."

It was the first word I understood. Wasps. I knew what WASP meant, but all I could think about was the time Dad and I had spent one whole afternoon routing the wasps from under our patio step back in Lanesport. After he had smoked them out, he showed me how they gathered mud to fashion their snug little nest holes. Only Dad didn't call them wasps. He said they were mud daubers. These people were not talking about mud daubers.

The Dakotan from the reservation finally got up and left the chair next to mine vacant. I looked up from all the shoes and saw Mrs. Enomoto moving through the crowd; seeing the chair, she sat down beside me.

"So you're looking for your family?"

I wondered what else Ernie had told her about me.

"I guess so," I answered. "I'm looking for my *father's* family. He's dead. I have a dad but no real father." It didn't make sense, but she seemed to understand. "My mother is not Japanese. My father was disowned for marrying her. As Ernie says, I'm a Hapa."

I couldn't tell if she thought that was nice or if that made me some sort of mistake.

Some people you are comfortable with. I was not comfortable with Mrs. Enomoto. She was overpolite and smiled too often, a smile that looked as fakey as mine felt, and when she asked a question she made me tell more than I wanted to. Teachers are good at that.

"You say the name is Yogushi?"

I had not said the name was Yogushi, but I nodded and smiled back, wondering if Ernie had put out an information bulletin on me.

"Maybe I can help you . . . if you like." Her smile flashed on and then off again like a neon sign.

I didn't answer right away, and she noticed.

"I have access to names of families from Sacramento who were interned, if it would help."

"I don't know if they were interned. They must have been, though. I really don't know much about them."

"Most people from here were sent to Tule Lake, or do you think some of your family may have gone back to Japan? Many did in forty-three."

"I don't know."

I didn't know, and right then I didn't much care. It was the same old war. I looked around, hoping Ernie would come and rescue me.

"I have to go north this week to take some books and supplies to one of our branch schools. It's not too much farther on up to Tule Lake. Would you like to ride along with me?"

"What do you think I could find out there?"

"I'm not sure, but I do think, Kimi, you could find *something!*" She was not smiling. "If it's all right with Ernie's mother," she smiled again, "how about Wednesday? We'll have to start early and we'll be late getting back."

I didn't want to go. I wanted to go home. It's funny but when you're home, you think you're buried in the middle of nowhere. Then when you go somewhere, that nowhere becomes the somewhere you most want to be. I didn't know how to tell Mrs. Enomoto all that, so I said, "Sure. I'll go." I'd take a couple of my books along to kill time on the trip.

"And," she added, "you might want to look at some of Barbara's books on Tule Lake. It'll make the trip more interesting."

Jav would have gone into hysterics. She would never believe that I had agreed to go on an all-day trip with a teacher who made Miss Sturm look like a cupcake.

Ernie thought the trip was a marvelous idea. Barbara was ecstatic. Maybe they were getting tired of me and were glad to get rid of me for a day.

EIGHT

The house was empty when I walked into the kitchen the next morning and found a note from Barbara on the kitchen table.

> *Hope you slept late this morning. I'll be home early.*
> *Left some books on my desk that you might want to*
> *look at.*

I sat looking out the window at the patio. It was another bright day, and the sunlight through the palm trees made patterns of shadows that moved with the breeze. I didn't feel like doing anything at all but sitting and staring at the day. I didn't even want to think, but that's impossible not to do. Even if you're thinking about not thinking, something is going on in your head.

It wasn't time to call Davey. Jav wasn't home so I couldn't talk to her. For a minute I thought of calling home just to hear the phone ring there. That was silly, though; all I had to do was to get on a plane and I'd *be* home. Maybe that was it. I'd call the airport and find out when there was a flight the next day and I'd ask Ernie to tell Mrs. Enomoto that I couldn't go with her.

And I'd try very, very hard to forget the name Yogushi.

I knew that was impossible, too, unless I never looked in a mirror again. It was crazy. Looking out through my eyes, I was Kim Andrews, but the person looking back at me would be Kimi Yogushi as long as I lived.

I was thinking of getting myself some breakfast when the phone rang. At first I wondered if I should answer it, but then I figured it might be Barbara or Ernie calling to see if I were all right. But when I said hello there was only silence and then the sound of a phone being hung up. Probably a wrong number.

The morning was too pretty for me to stay inside, and by this time tomorrow I could be on my way to chilly Iowa. I'd borrow Barbara's swimsuit again and spend an hour or so in the sun, and then I'd call the airport. And I'd even look at the books Barbara had left me. I didn't have to read them, but if she asked me about them, I wouldn't have to lie. I stretched out on the chaise longue, stacking Barbara's books beside the chair.

First, though, I'd start *Sweet Memories.* I hadn't finished *Cheers for Cathy*, but that was one of the nice things about those books. I could switch back and forth right in the middle of any of them and hardly even notice. Names, hair color, and eyes changed, but mostly all the stories were the same. At least they weren't like Davey's fantasies.

"What did he write?" Carrie screamed, as Wendi clutched her yearbook with both arms.

"I haven't looked yet!" Wendi said, tossing her bright blond hair. She closed her dark blue eyes for a second as if in a trance.

Randy had signed her yearbook just under his picture —not only signed it, but written something, too. It couldn't have taken him five minutes just to spell his name, could it?

Something was wrong. Maybe it was the slant of the sunlight across the page. Maybe it was the warmth of the morning, but I didn't feel a part of the book. Usually I could slide right into whoever's head was on the page— Lisa, Candi, Muffie—but not this morning. I'd close my eyes and try again later. The sun was just as warm as it had looked, and the sky was so blue it almost hurt my eyes when I opened them again. I wished Jav were with me, or Davey, even. Tomorrow I'd see him. I'd even eat sauerkraut pizza and pretend to like it.

Next week spring vacation would be over. I'd be home and so would Mom and Dad. School would start again, and these days in Sacramento would be just a little gap in time, a blank to everyone except me. I could tell Davey and Jav about it, but they'd never know what it was really like because they hadn't lived through it with me. It was almost like those books—stepping into another world for a while.

I reached down and took one of Barbara's books from the top of the stack. It was a skinny paperback that wouldn't take long to get through. *Executive Order 9066.* The title wasn't interesting, but under it a face stared out. It was a child, maybe six or seven, and she wasn't looking at me or even at whoever had taken her picture. It was more as if she were looking past the photographer at something she didn't understand.

She was Japanese, and something like a shipping tag hung from her coat. She looked enough like me to *be* me. I wasn't sure I wanted to open the book. I did, though, after a long while, and entered still another new world.

The book was mostly pictures of people, people of all ages, men and women, boys and girls—all of them Japanese . . . Japanese-Americans and it was World War II, and for the first time I saw the camps—the concentration camps. They were bleak and ugly, the faces sad and confused and angry.

It took me a long time to look at all the pictures, and when I finished, I started all over again from the beginning, this time reading the words. Every time I saw a photograph of a little boy, I wondered if he could have been my father. And my grandparents—were they the couple standing waiting to be taken away?

As I finally closed the book and put it down, I heard a door open behind me. I turned, expecting to see Ernie or Barbara, but instead a man was walking toward me. For just a second I was confused; it was as if one of the pictures

I'd been looking at had come to life—only his face was smiling.

"I hope I didn't frighten you," he said. "I'm Barbara's husband. You must be Kimi."

"No. I mean, no, you didn't frighten me, and yes, I'm Kimi Yogushi."

So much for forgetting that name! I knew I was staring, but I couldn't help it. He was a small, handsome man in a sports jacket, and he could have been my father.

"I was in Washington, but I left early."' He pulled up a chair and sat down. "I have to be in San Francisco to testify at the Reparation Hearings."

"Oh." I pretended I understood.

"The Government is beginning to understand that it owes a debt to Japanese-American citizens who were imprisoned during the war." He looked around. "Where's everybody?"

"Ernie's at his school, and Barbara said she'd be back early, but I'm not sure when that is." I thought I should explain myself, but then I decided that he must know all about me since he obviously knew my name.

"Barb's 'early' is usually at least two hours later than she intends. Ernie's, too, for that matter. Me? I'm always early. Have you found out anything about your family?"

I didn't know why—maybe because I was missing home or maybe because of the book I'd been looking at or maybe because he was a father, even if he wasn't my father, but I found myself telling him everything that had happened including the last address I'd found and my decision that morning to go back home. "And then I read this book, and now I'm not sure anymore."

For a minute or two he didn't say anything, instead sat quietly watching me as if waiting for me to go on. I couldn't. I didn't have anything left to say. I realized that I'd probably never talked that long, that seriously to anyone, not even Jav. Mr. Okamura was a complete stranger except for the one thing that my mind kept sliding back to. He could have been my father.

"Kimi," he said slowly, looking down at his hands and then at the cloudless sky, "I think I know . . . well . . . I think I know a little of what you are feeling. The pull in two different directions. For me it was my grandparents." He stopped as if considering what he was going to say next.

"Your grandparents?" I asked, wanting him to keep talking.

"I was very young, only six, but I remember them. My grandfather gave orders; my grandmother obeyed. It was part of her tradition to obey. It was in nineteen-forty when they went back."

"To Japan?"

"To Nagasaki."

"Were they there when . . . ?" I didn't know whether to say "we" or "they" dropped the bomb.

"Yes, they died with the others. And for a long time I

126

didn't know who to hate—Japan for beginning the war or America for the bomb."

"At least you had your mother and father," I said. "You knew who they were and who you were."

He stood up. "That, too, took time after the war began. We were American citizens. We knew we were loyal. Then why were we forced from our homes? Why were we held in a stall at a racetrack? Why were we put on a train with windows covered? And why," his voice was harsh, "why were we sent to the camp at Manzanar for nearly four years?"

I couldn't begin to answer any of his questions, and I wasn't sure that he even remembered I was sitting there. Maybe I wasn't the only one who moved in and out of worlds and time. Maybe that was what being an adult meant—that you remembered things you'd rather forget.

He smiled at me then and said, "I'm sorry, Kimi. I didn't realize I still held that much anger. I thought I'd come to terms with it long ago. Perhaps you *are* right to forget about your search and the past."

"You mean what I *don't* know can't hurt."

"Something like that, I suppose. You're young. You are untouched by all that happened. You have a home and a family far away from here. You may be happier if you never know more than you do now. But," he said, turning toward the house, "you are certainly welcome here as long as you want to stay. Now I must hurry. Tell Barbara I'll call her this evening. And Kimi, good luck, whatever you decide to do."

I thanked him and said good-bye. When I heard the patio door slide shut, I picked up the book again and looked at the child on the cover. She was young, younger than I, and she had had no choice at all . . . and I was pretty sure her memories were not sweet.

It took another couple of hours, but I skimmed through all the books Barbara had left for me. Here was a whole history I'd never seen before, written by Japanese-Americans about Japanese-Americans in the camps. Was this what my father "wouldn't—or couldn't" talk about even with my mother?

I heard the phone ring and ran into the house to answer, but when I picked up the receiver and said hello, there was silence again, and whoever it was hung up. At first I was a little scared. Maybe someone knew I was alone in the house, and maybe they were going to come and . . . that was silly! Davey's monsters weren't real, especially on a sunny day.

The phone book was on the counter, so I looked up the airline number. I'd check on flights out, but I'd wait until after I talked to Davey.

I placed the call at exactly six o'clock. Davey answered. "If this is Sybil, this is Davey who is not here. At the tone, please leave a message."

It was Davey, and he *was* there. It was another of his crazy games. I waited until Davey said, "Bleep. Bleep."

"Listen, Toad. I know you're there. And you're being dweeblier than ever." I went ahead and told him about Mrs. Enomoto and the trip to Tule and about Mr. Okamura. I waited for Davey to talk, but he kept pretending he was an answering service. He must have been holding the phone away from his mouth, for I couldn't even hear him breathing.

It was too dumb a trick even for Davey to play and really irresponsible on a long-distance call, but Davey could make fun out of anything.

Nothing but silence. It was a waste of my phone call, like talking to a lampshade. At least I knew he was listening because he giggled and bleeped before he hung up. It was the dumbest thing he'd done since the day—three years ago—he spent two hours pretending to be a parking meter and not talking unless someone put a nickel in his pocket.

Ernie walked in just as I hung up the phone.

"Hi, Kimi. Did you have a good day?"

Teachers who hand back papers with smiley faces on them instead of grades and people who say, "Have a good day" make me want to scream. Ernie's was a question though, not an order.

"Better than tomorrow. I'm going to Tule Lake with Mrs. Enomoto."

"I know that. You promised her last night."

"Well—there are promises. . . ."

"And promises?" Ernie finished for me.

"It's easy to make promises. . . ." I began.

"Hard to keep them."

I felt like a ventriloquist's dummy.

"And sometimes you're not even honest with yourself."

"How do you know?" I asked.

"Look." He held up both arms. "I'm human, too. Sometimes I tell the truth and wish I hadn't. Sometimes I don't and wish I had." He looked at me for a long time and finally said, "Kimi, honesty doesn't have anything to do with being Japanese or Hapa or" . . . I knew he was trying not to laugh . . . "an Iowan from Lanesport."

I looked down at my jeans. They needed washing. And my sneakers, too. Justin Waterford in *Justin for Jenny* didn't talk that way to Jenny when he was trying to explain to her that just because she had red hair and a powdering of freckles across the bridge of her nose, it wouldn't keep her from being Homecoming Queen. Justin gazed into her eyes and brushed her hand. Ernie sat on the corner of the desk, swinging his legs and twirling a pencil. Me? I would have gladly settled for freckles and red hair.

"It's not how you look on the outside," Ernie went on. "It's how you look *out* from the inside."

He was at least half right. I was going to Tule Lake because of *Executive Order* 9066 and the face of a girl who might have been me.

NINE

A scrim of early-morning fog hid the mountains and spread a veil of mist across the valley as I stepped out the front door.

"I'm glad to see you're ready," Mrs. Enomoto said, as I climbed into the front seat.

"I woke up early."

"It's a Japanese trait, being early for an appointment. I think it's bred into our genes."

It certainly was not bred into *my* genes. I was always the last of our family to get ready for anything.

We drove through empty streets, the car lights glittering against the wet pavement.

"We call this Tule fog. It comes down from the north, but it disappears with the rising sun."

"I hope so."

"Sacramento is full of history, you know. Over there is Discovery Park. You can't see it very well, but you must visit it while you're here. Our rivers run together there: the American and the Sacramento."

"Oh," I mumbled. I wasn't interested in a geography lesson that early in the morning, but I tried to sound enthusiastic.

"I hope this day will prove instructive for you, Kimi."

Mrs. Enomoto was a teacher, all right. Jav says teachers go to college to learn how to talk and they come out with a language of objectives, goal-oriented units, and three-phase approaches.

I scrunched down in the seat and wondered how I was going to endure the hours ahead. Mostly Mrs. Enomoto talked and I grunted and nodded and looked out at the scenery, which wasn't very interesting. After a long pause, she started on some story about one of her pupils, and I didn't think she was ever going to find her way to the end. I amused myself by seeing how long I could hold my breath. I think I fell asleep then.

After we stopped for gas and breakfast and were on our way, Mrs. Enomoto started in again in the same precise tone. At first I thought she was still talking about success-oriented environments for instructional activities, so I was only half listening when she said, "There were Yogushis at Tule Lake during the war."

"There were!" I almost shouted.

"A mother, father, a girl, and a boy."

"What were their first names?" I held my breath.

"The father's name was Yoki."

"Are you sure?"

"I'm sure. I didn't know the family there, however. After all, more than eighteen thousand of us were imprisoned at Tule Lake."

"You were in prison, too?"

"Yes."

"You mean for...."

"For being born," she said, her mouth barely opening to say the words. "Four years. Twelve when I went in and sixteen when I got out."

"You were my age!"

"Yes." Her voice was flat. "Your age."

"Was it awful?" I thought of my father, a little boy in prison.

"So awful that I've only been able to talk about it since I met Barbara and some of the others like me."

"Barbara?"

"She was born in a camp in Arkansas."

"They took people from California all the way to Arkansas?"

"Yes. To a place called Jerome that doesn't even exist on the map, doesn't have an address. I met Barbara when she was trying to get a birth certificate. She couldn't get one because she was told there was no such place as Jerome."

"Isn't there? I mean now."

"No."

"So if someone asked Barbara where she was born, she'd have to say Nowhere."

"That's right. Nowhere. As far as most Americans were concerned, camps didn't exist."

We were driving through flat desertlike land, and it seemed as if it had been miles since we'd passed through a town.

"Going back to Tule Lake is a kind of pilgrimage for me. You see, Kimi, we can carry our Japanese heritage with pride or we can hide it in shame. That's why I asked you to come along today."

"But I'm just half and half."

"We're all half and half. I was as American in nineteen-forty-two as any other teen-ager. Spoke English. Poured nickels into jukeboxes. Hoped when I got into high school to be a cheerleader. That was important in my day. Thank goodness, girls think of other things now."

Obviously Mrs. Enomoto hadn't read *Cheers for Cathy*.

"Is Tule Lake in California?" I finally asked.

"Just barely. It's on the Oregon border."

Rats! Here I was wasting a whole day. What did Mrs. Enomoto expect me to find at Tule Lake? Footprints in the sand? I was searching for my father. What could I possibly find in an old prison camp?

"What did you do at Tule Lake all those years? Fish? Swim?"

"It was sink or swim when I was there. I learned to swim."

"Oh." It was obvious she didn't want to talk anymore.

We delivered the books and supplies at a school. I helped Mrs. Enomoto carry the boxes in, and at lunch, when the waitress asked, "What would your daughter like?" I answered, "A cheeseburger," without feeling anything was wrong.

At Tule Lake, everything was wrong. I expected to see something, but there was nothing to see, not even a lake. We drove out into a field of stuff that looked like rows of horseradish.

"This is it?" I asked, looking around at the acres of rows that stretched across a valley. At one side the fields curved around what looked like a small airport. In the distance was a hill that might have been a mountain ages ago. A cold wind swept across the field, swirling sand against our ankles. I shivered and glanced at Mrs. Enomoto. I had ridden all day to tramp around a field?

With her eyes fixed on the hill, Mrs. Enomoto began to walk down the cultivated rows, leaves slapping against her legs. I followed. She did not speak until we came to what looked from a distance like a gravestone. The path leading to it was lined with rocks and stones, and as we came nearer, I could see it was not a gravestone but a monument.

"Read what it says." Mrs. Enomoto pointed to the bronze plate.

I shaded my eyes from the glare of the sun and read aloud:

Tule Lake was one of ten American concentration camps
established during World War II to incarcerate 110,000
persons of Japanese ancestry, of whom the majority were
American citizens, behind barbed wire and guard towers,
without charge, trial or establishment of guilt. These
camps are reminders of how racism, economic and politi-
cal exploitation and expediency can undermine the con-
stitutional guarantees of United States citizens and aliens
alike. May the injustices and humiliation suffered here
never recur.

I looked across the valley, remembering the rows of
tarpaper barracks I had seen in Barbara's books, the guard
towers, the barbed-wire fence, the armed soldiers, and a
little boy who might have been my father, imprisoned
because his skin was colored and his eyes a different shape.

"It isn't much to look at, is it?" An old man in a red
plaid shirt, pant legs tucked into heavy boots, walked
toward us. He tipped his billed cap, pulling it up from
the back of his head, then tugging it down on his forehead.

"It's enough," Mrs. Enomoto said, smiling her smile
that was never quite a smile.

"It was a lot different once, I tell you. I've lived around
here all my life. I can remember when there was more
people here than anywhere else in the county."

Mrs. Enomoto did not comment.

"All that's left is that migrant workers' camp over there
beyond the fence. They still use some of the same old
barracks."

"Are they locked up, too?" I asked.

"No." He scuffed at the sand with the toe of his boot. "They have to get out to work. They follow the harvests and move on."

"They are not locked up, Kimi," Mrs. Enomoto said, "but they're locked into a way of life for many of the same reasons that we were—economic reasons. We were sent to the camps because of our Japanese heritage, even though we were American citizens, but that crime of imprisonment had its roots in a century of hatred toward us because we were an economic threat. The 'Yellow Peril' they called us. We worked hard, we succeeded, and we were imprisoned. Isn't that right?"

"Wouldn't know about that." The man tugged at his cap. "All I know is that the migrants need the work. We need the hands. Isn't that the way the world works?"

For the first time since I'd met her, Mrs. Enomoto frowned.

"Over there's the old power plant. They still use that, but they tore down the guard tower a few years back. Made it into that hangar on the airstrip."

I looked at the airplane hangar, across at the barracks, and back to the power plant, trying to make a picture that would fit those in Barbara's books.

"It's all gone!" I said. "As though it was never here. As though it never happened."

"It happened," Mrs. Enomoto said.

The man glanced at her, then turned away, squinting

up into the sun. "I wasn't in the war," he said, as if someone had asked. "Farmers were deferred. They needed us to grow food, so we grew it. We did what we were told back then."

"So did we," Mrs. Enomoto added.

"That's all in the past, lady. We all have to forget."

"Perhaps you have to forget." Mrs. Enomoto smiled politely. "We must remember."

"Suppose so." The man readjusted his cap. "Well, I've got to get going. Got to check my fields. We need rain bad up here."

We walked away in opposite directions.

"It's so quiet," I remarked. "So peaceful."

"Now, yes. Then . . . then it was . . . no privacy, alcoholism, secrets, craziness, sickness, food poisoning, fear, shooting, shouting, families disintegrating, and wind . . . always wind blowing through the tar paper and we had to huddle close or freeze. . . ."

Mrs. Enomoto's voice was fierce.

"Dust, bad milk, no seasoning, no tea, and of all things, they served us rice pudding. You can't do that to rice! Fighting—fighting for food and supplies and space and hiding treasures away and children running wild and parents giving up on discipline." She stopped to catch a breath. "Yes, Kimi, it's peaceful now." She looked up at the hill. "This camp erased a part of my life! People have to know we were here. People must know that in erasing these camps they have destroyed our history. For forty years we have carried this awful anger. Do you want to see how we lived?" Mrs. Enomoto paced off a square among the rows.

It wasn't much bigger than my bedroom at home.

"That was your room?"

"That was for all six of us. When Father registered, after Pearl Harbor, we were given twelve tags. A tag went on each of our suitcases and the others on our coat lapels—tags with no names, just numbers. We were no longer Ochidas. We were family #8659.

I had read about German camps where people were numbered.

"Did you have schools?"

"Yes. But at first only our teacher had a chair. We sat on the floor." She turned and we started walking back to the car. "I remember one morning when we had finished the Pledge of Allegiance and started singing 'My country 'tis of thee, sweet land of liberty,' and when I got to the word *liberty* I started to cry.

"The teacher sent me to the barracks that day. We learned in school. We learned typing and we didn't have a typewriter. The teacher drew little circles on pieces of paper, and we practiced by touching our fingers to the make-believe keys."

The wind blew across the lake bed, sending another shower of sand whirling around us.

"What was it like when you got out?"

"Sad in many ways. We had to start over again. We'd

lost everything. Mother washed dishes in a Chinese restaurant. We girls worked as waitresses. My brothers and father did yard work. They say to forget is to forgive. I cannot do either."

I turned and looked once again across the Tule Lake Camp. Sunlight glowed above the hill, spilling color down across the fields. I started to get in the car, but Mrs. Enomoto stood, eyes closed, murmuring over and over words I couldn't understand.

As we drove away, I asked her what the words meant that she had said.

"It's a kind of Buddhist amen. My father taught it to me. When you are sad, if you recite the words, your sadness fades."

"Will you teach them to me?"

"Someday, perhaps. Why don't you get into the backseat and take a nap. It's a long way back and you've had a full day."

Usually, to get to sleep, I pretend to be the Cathy or Angela or Karen from one of those books. It didn't work this time. Mrs. Enomoto's memories were more real than Karen's in *Love Memories*.

I finally sat up and said, "Mrs. Enomoto. When you were sixteen in the camp, what did you want to do?"

"Run!" she said without turning her head, but I saw her glance up at me in the rearview mirror.

"But you didn't."

"No, Kimi, I didn't. You grow up when you learn that life is cause and effect—that what you do has consequences."

I tried to sleep away the miles, but with thinking about cause and effect, truth and consequences, Tule Lake and Lanesport, and growing up and going home, I might as well have stayed in the front seat and listened to Mrs. Enomoto.

TEN

I was so tired I was seeing double by the time we got back and I pulled out my futon in the early-morning hours—tired of running, tired of seeking, tired of pretending to be Kim in Lanesport and Kimi in Sacramento. Ernie said my trouble was that I couldn't be honest with myself. Maybe Nez was right, checking off "inconsistent behavior" on all my orange slips. How could I be consistent when I wasn't like anybody else I knew?

I thought about Mrs. Enomoto when she was my age at Tule Lake, and right then I knew, as sure as my name was Kim Andrews—or Kimi Yogushi—or whatever—that my history paper for Mr. Mitchell was going to be about Family #8659 at Tule Lake. I'd pretend that I was Kenji Yogushi, a little American boy growing up in an American prison camp during World War II, but I couldn't write the paper unless I found out more.

The next morning, I dug out the second address that I'd found in the 1952 telephone directory and spread out the city map. The street wasn't too far away—two or three miles, maybe. I could call a taxi . . . or walk . . . but there were a couple of bicycles in the garage, and Barbara had said to make myself at home. I found a bike, a balloon-tired, one-speed Schwinn, practically an antique, but it had wheels and pedals.

I've always loved riding a bike. Maybe because it's so wonderful to move without noise. Sailing's the same way when the wind catches the sails and you move without any sound except the keel slicing through water. On a bike, all you hear is the hum of tires on pavement. Davey told me once that bicycles were the reason people started to improve roads. Davey has more answers than there are questions.

After a mile or two, I knew this part of the city could have used some improvement, for as I ticked off the blocks, the streets became narrower and I was busy trying to avoid potholes. It was definitely a neighborhood to go *from* rather than go *to*: rows and rows of little houses with patches of scrubby lawns squeezed in between. I found the house . . . a tiny box, but surely not the right house for my father's family. I checked the address again. It *was* the right house. How could they have lived in such a place? Not that it was dirty. It just looked poor and tired.

The old man who answered my knock looked the same. He might have been Chicano or even Filipino, I couldn't tell.

"Yah," he grunted, holding the door open just enough to poke his head through. His eyes were deep brown beneath thick gray hair. I decided I wouldn't lie. He looked as if he had been lied to many, many times.

"I wonder if you could help me," I began.

"You lost?" He looked at my bicycle.

"No. I'm looking for someone."

"You live around here?" He stepped down to the sidewalk. There was no porch, only a wooden step.

"No. But I'm looking for someone who lived here once, I think. In this house. I'm Japanese."

I did not say "American."

"Guessed that," he grunted.

"My grandfather. I think he lived here once."

"Your grandfather? You must mean Yoki."

I couldn't even repeat the name. When you're looking and hoping for something and you find it, it's so surprising you can't talk. You can only feel.

"Yoki . . . Yogushi." I thought I'd never get the name out.

"Yep. Yogushi."

"You knew him?"

"Bought this place from his missus, after he died. When she moved in with her married daughter."

Could I have an aunt *and* a grandmother?

"Would . . . would you know the daughter's name?" I felt as if I were coming in on the last lap of a long race.

"Don't do names very good. That was years ago. I do remember the old woman didn't speak English. The young one did all the talking. They'd had a rough time, coming back from them camps. Killed old Yoki. I helped him with things now and then. I lived down the street."

"Do you know where they moved? Where the daughter lives?"

"Don't know. Somewhere in the city, I think." He sat down on the step.

I propped my bike against the house and sat down beside him. "If you think real hard, do you suppose you could think of her name?"

"Not sure. Japanese names sound alike. It was sort of like Yogushi, but it didn't have the *shi* on it."

"Did they have other children, maybe, who lived here?"

He scratched the back of his neck. "Not when I knew them. Just Yoki and the missus."

"Wasn't there a boy?"

"Could have been. They kept to themselves. Only one I ever met was Nomi. That was it! Nomi! Funny, I couldn't think of that before."

"Nomi," I repeated.

I could see myself calling every Japanese in the Sacramento phone book and asking for Nomi.

"They your family, you say? How'd you lose track of them?"

"My father died before I was born. I was adopted by another family."

It was only half of the truth, but sometimes the whole truth takes too long.

"I see." He spat, spreading his knees apart and grinding

145

the wetness under the heel of his shoe. "I might have some old papers in the house here. Seems to me there was something from that daughter when I bought the place. I'll go see, if you want to wait."

I sat on the step and waited. A tired-looking dog, as tired as the neighborhood, waddled across the yard, sniffed at my sneakers, looked up at me, and flopped down at my feet.

"Nice fella," I said, scratching behind his ears. He had long Cocker ears and the tiny body of a terrier. The dog yawned and licked my hand. He belonged, I could tell, with the house.

The brown envelope was addressed to Juan Verenzo. I hadn't even asked the man's name, but there are times when names don't matter—just the people behind them. In the upper left corner was a name . . . and an address! Mrs. C. L. Ozaki. There was no need to copy them down. I could never forget.

"This is from her. You're sure?"

"That's her. It's what you wanted, isn't it?"

"Oh, yes." I stood up. "Oh, Mr. Verenzo, you don't know what you've done for me." I shook his hand with both of mine. I don't think anyone had touched him for a long time.

The streets weren't half as narrow and bumpy as they had been before as I pedaled as fast as my legs could pump back to Barbara's. I had an aunt. Maybe a grandmother, and I knew just what they looked like. They looked like me!

When I got back, I ran into the den and thumbed through the telephone directory. Ozaki. It was there, and the address matched the address I had memorized at one glance. Sturm would have given me A in attentiveness.

I sat down and tried to catch my breath. I had found them! I closed my eyes, opened them and looked again at the page. The name was still there—C. L. Ozaki.

The longer I looked at it, the less friendly the name seemed. It didn't mean that my grandmother was alive, or even my aunt, for that matter. Maybe C. L. Ozaki was someone like the old bearded man I had seen on Barbara's tour of Sacramento. Just because the name and the address were the same as on the envelope didn't mean that the person who lived there would understand who I was or care. I couldn't just turn up on the doorstep with a picture in my hand and a story about its being pinned to my blanket at the orphanage. That had been a dumb lie the first time. Even with variation, it couldn't work twice.

I had to go to that house and meet whoever lived there, but I didn't want to do it the wrong way, and I didn't know a right way. Mrs. Enomoto! She'd know what I should do. I was sure she'd spent most of her life doing exactly the right thing at the right time. That's probably how she'd learned her smile. Besides, she was a teacher, and teachers knew things like that.

I wheeled the bike out of the garage again. If this kept up, I'd have calves as big as posts. I flew down streets that were becoming familiar to me, made the correct turns, and pulled up in front of the school. Classes were still in session. I pulled open the glass door. All schools smell alike—of sweat, sweeping compound, and the day's hot lunch. They all look alike too—main office, first floor just to the right of the entry.

"Would it be possible for me to see Mrs. Enomoto?" I asked the secretary when she finally looked up.

"She's in class now. Would you care to wait?"

"Yes. Thank you." I hated waiting. I had been waiting for almost two years.

"Who shall I say is here?"

"Kimi Yogushi." The name came out almost automatically.

The office was quiet except for the secretary's rhythmic typing. I could barely stand the quietness. I studied every picture on the wall, rearranged them in my mind and re-hung them. I counted the tiles in the floor and estimated the length and width of the waiting room. Eleven feet by nine—if the tiles were nine inches square. The ceiling was twelve feet high. I tried to repeat the sonnet we were supposed to memorize for Miss Turner the week before in Lanesport:

When to the sessions of sweet silent thought
I summon up remembrances of things past. . . .

I couldn't get past the "past." I was saying the alphabet backwards when Mrs. Enomoto walked in.

"Why, Kimi, what is it?"

I must have looked like a windblown rice field after my bicycle marathon.

"I found them!"

I didn't mean to shout, but the secretary stopped typing and peered over the divider.

"You've spoken to them?" Mrs. Enomoto's eyes widened.

"Not yet. I had to talk to you first."

"Good. Good." Taking my arm, she steered me down the hall and into a tiny room, her office.

"I didn't know what to do next," I tried to explain. "I thought maybe you'd know and could help me."

"Correct. Very wise." She nodded toward a chair and I sat down.

"Now, Kimi," she said, arranging the papers on her desk into neat piles. "If I understand the situation, I think we must go about this very carefully. If, as you tell me, your father was disowned when he married your mother, the family must be of the old school."

"Yes," I agreed, wishing she'd forget the speech and get on with our plans.

"That means we must take a formal approach."

I had only two days left in Sacramento, and the formal approach sounded about as promising as Mom's "maybe someday, Kimi."

"It may be hard for you to understand the importance of formality," Mrs. Enomoto continued. "Before the war, we Japanese-Americans attempted to maintain our own culture by being inconspicuous, working hard, and proving we were loyal citizens. It didn't work. We were strange birds in a flock."

I was not interested in birds. I wanted to know how I could meet my family.

"When we were taken from our homes and put into camps, we Nisei—those of us who were born here—were really more American than Japanese, but you see, our faces made the difference. Because we looked like the enemy, we became the enemy. Many at Tule Lake clung to their heritage, while still remaining loyal Americans. Now your family...."

At last she was getting to my family.

"I think your family held firm to their Japanese culture —the samurai pride, the reserve, you know. That means you must approach them properly."

"How do you mean?"

I saw myself in a kimono, carrying a fan like Madam Butterfly.

"We must call first and make an appointment."

"What'll I say?"

"Perhaps it would be better if I were to call. I could say that as a teacher here, I have met someone who might have a close association with the Yogushi family."

"Oh, yes. I think you should call," I said quickly.

I was relieved she wasn't going to insist that I make the phone call. It's hard to talk to people when you can't see their faces.

"They will probably assume you have some tie to their past."

I did!

"I will ask if they will see you. I will tell them that your name is Kimi.

"Andrews or Yogushi?"

"I think it will be best to say Andrews. It will be up to you to explain. When do you want to see them?"

"Tomorrow?" I suggested.

"Fine. I'll call this evening."

I stood up. I thought we were through.

"But, Kimi, there are several other things. A gift, for instance. A small little something—appropriate for the family. And a few little courtesies. Would you have some time this evening? I could make the call when I go home, perhaps agree on a time—two, maybe, tomorrow afternoon. I can stop by and let you know for sure and then, perhaps, you and I can have a dress rehearsal."

"I didn't bring a dress."

She laughed, sort of. "I didn't mean it that way. I mean we might go over how you will act. You may look Japanese, but you have a few things to learn. However, we can remedy that, at least enough for the time being."

"You mean an etiquette lesson?"

Mom would have gone into parental shock!

"A lesson in Issei etiquette."

"Issei etiquette?"

"First-generation Japanese-Americans, born in Japan."

Issei, Nisei, Sansei, Yansei ran through my mind.

"I'll stop by for you about seven. All right?"

It *was* all right! Everything was turning out all right, and Mrs. Enomoto, even if she was sort of teachery, was Grade-A-All-Right. I wanted to tell her that. Instead I blurted out like a dummy, "How come you're so nice to me? I mean, I hardly know you, and yet you've gone out of your way to help."

She began sorting through the stack of papers. "I suppose it's the teacher in me—wanting to help someone learn, and you're so determined. You're right, of course. The more we learn about ourselves, the better we know ourselves, and in turn understand others."

I was dismissed. That was one thing I *had* learned from the sessions with Sturm back in Lanesport, my dismissal line.

Usually, when I see a school hall stretching ahead of me, I want to run. Probably because it's the one big no-no in every school in the nation. This time I was not tempted. I walked slowly down the hall, thinking. As I got on the bike and started back, it occurred to me that Mrs. Enomoto had not exactly answered my last question. She had avoided it so neatly that I'd almost forgotten I'd asked it. Instead she had delivered a pat little speech.

I pedaled along, barely keeping my balance as I steered the bike close to the curb. Mrs. Enomoto had spent a whole day with me at Tule Lake, but maybe Ernie had talked her into that. She was the one who had found out that the Yogushis had been sent there, and now she was going to call for me and make an appointment. Of course, I went to her for help, but she needn't have gone to the bother of seeing that I wouldn't goof up my first visit. Why? Was it because I was Japanese? Half Japanese, that is.

I was going to ask Barbara, but there was another one of her notes saying she'd be gone until nine. Ernie rushed in—and out—saying, "Tell Mom I'll be back later."

There was nothing to do but call Davey. I had to talk to someone. He would certainly be at Mrs. Mueller's.

"Yes?" It *was* Mrs. Mueller! Of all people, I didn't want to talk to her.

"It's Kim . . . ." I almost said Kimi.

"Oh, Kim," she cried in sort of a surprised tone that I didn't believe. "How are you? Is everything going according to plan? Are you all right?"

"Fine," I answered, trying to answer her questions in order. "Everything's fine, and yes, everything's going according to plan. Is Davey there?"

"Nooo." There was a long pause when I could hear

153

funny little noises in the background. "But . . . he should be coming in . . . any minute now. Shall I have him call you?"

"Please, Mrs. Mueller. I'll give you my number."

"We have the number, dear, remember? I'll have him call the very second he gets back. All right?"

"Fine. Thanks."

"You'll be coming home soon, won't you?"

"In a day or so. According to the plan. Be sure and tell Davey to call just as soon as he comes in."

"I certainly will, Kim."

I thought Davey would never call. I waited and waited and kept looking out the window hoping Mrs. Enomoto wouldn't come too early, even though it was "bred in her genes."

"Kimi? It's me, Davey." He sounded as if he'd just come in from running around the block.

"Where have you been? I thought you'd never call back."

"I was just over—I mean—outside with some of the guys. Why?"

"You're all out of breath. Anyway, you won't believe what I've found out."

"You mean you found them. You're going to go see them?"

"How do you know?"

"I guessed."

154

"Anyway, there's an aunt, and I'm going to see her tomorrow."

"Super! When are you coming home?"

"Saturday. How are things there?"

"No problem. We're all going to meet you at the airport."

"What do you mean all?"

"You know. Me and Mrs. Mueller . . . and Jav. . . ."

"I thought Jav was in Colorado."

"Oh. That's right. Spider's coming down though."

Davey was not telling the truth. I knew it.

"What about Mom and Dad? Have you talked to them?"

"A couple of times. . . ."

"Did you cover for me?"

"Of course. Told them you were over at Jav's one time, and the next time I said you were out jogging."

"Davey! I don't jog."

"Well, anyway, I told them something. I don't remember."

"And they'll be back Sunday, won't they?"

"Sure. Didn't I tell you everything is working out super?"

I hung up. Davey was a genius with generalities, but he was lousy with specifics.

Mrs. Enomoto arrived a few minutes later.

"I thought maybe we could drive around, locate the

address, and then go up to my apartment. We won't be disturbed there."

"Did you call them?" I knew I should have waited at least half a second before I bombarded her with questions, but I couldn't.

"Yes," she said, moving the lever slowly into drive. Mrs. Enomoto drove as carefully and precisely as she talked. "I called as soon as I returned home," she went on. "Mrs. Ozaki will see you tomorrow . . . at two."

"What did she sound like?"

"Polite. Proper."

"Did she . . . did she seem sort of interested?"

"It's hard to tell. She was gracious, if that is what you mean."

"But she knows I'm coming?"

Mrs. Enomoto glanced over at me. "She knows *someone* is coming. I didn't hint at your age."

"She could think someone real old was coming. . . ."

"It will be better that way. You may be a shock to her at first, but I think . . . I hope—eventually a pleasant one."

It was the nicest thing Mrs. Enomoto had ever said to me. I looked straight ahead and grinned. I think she saw me.

The street was not too far from Barbara's. Within pedaling distance, I decided as we crept along looking at house numbers.

"There it is!" I cried as we drove slowly past a ranch-style brick, sitting back on an expanse of lawn.

"Observe it carefully," Mrs. Enomoto said. "I'll drive by again so you will be sure to recognize it tomorrow."

She didn't know that with one look I could have drawn the house in complete detail.

We drove by again. "I think it best that you go alone. You can pedal out here on your bike. Agreed?"

"Agreed," I agreed, but I didn't feel quite that agreeable. If I ever needed someone to go with me, it would be when I walked up to the front door and knocked—a door heavy with wood and beveled glass, with an iron grill across it.

Mrs. Enomoto's apartment, on the other hand, could have been cut out of a house-and-garden magazine. It felt like home, with glass doors that opened to a patio full of green plants and flowers.

We began the rehearsal of my visit at once. Mrs. Enomoto believed in schedules, I could tell. I practiced coming in the door, from her bedroom, introducing myself as the Kimi "about *whom* Mrs. Enomoto spoke yesterday," keeping my eyes lowered in respect to an elder, waiting patiently without looking around until I was invited to sit down, and sitting quietly until Mrs. Ozaki inquired about me further. We went through the whole thing at least five times until Mrs. Enomoto finally pronounced me satisfactory.

"Now, as I mentioned before, a small gift to present, probably just before you leave."

"A gift?" I had forgotten about the gift.

"Juse a little something."

"What about the picture?"

"Picture? What picture?" Mrs. Enomoto looked at me as if she'd caught me cheating on a worksheet.

"Didn't I tell you?" I tried to remember. "I guess I didn't, did I?"

"No, you didn't. You mean . . . a picture of . . . of your father." She was not looking at me, now. I *was* looking at her.

"Yes. And of my mom. Do you want to see it?" I reached for my purse.

"No." She stood up. "That will not be necessary." She walked out on the patio, rearranged a couple of her plants so that a spidery mass of waxy green no longer hid a delicate little yellow bloom, plucked off a few dead leaves, and finally said, her back toward me, "I don't know what to tell you about the picture. I'll have to leave that up to you. If you think the time is right, you might show it to them. You'll know when, I'm sure. If this picture is yours to give, it could be a lovely gift. A welcome gift, I should think. I'm not sure."

"It's all I have," I said.

She came back in from the patio, sat down for a while as if thinking of more things to tell me, then she stood up. "Would you care for some tea?"

"I don't know. I guess so."

"You must not answer Mrs. Ozaki that way tomorrow,"

she said in her teacher voice. "You must say, 'Yes. If you please.'"

So I drank tea from a thin little cup while sitting with *uncrossed* legs on a straight chair. If I were only half Japanese before, I felt totally Japanese by the time our lesson was over.

As we drove back to Barbara's, I said, more to make conversation than anything else, "I'm going home day after tomorrow, no matter what happens."

"Oh?" she said.

"Whether Mrs. Ozaki is glad to see me or not, at least I know I have a real family somewhere."

"You are very lucky, Kimi. You have two families. One in Lanesport and one here. Not everyone is that fortunate."

"I never thought of it that way," I replied as we turned into Barbara's drive. "But you've helped me so much. Do you help everyone like that?"

I was determined to make her answer the question she had avoided earlier. I crawled out of the car and held the door open.

"You're not everyone, Kimi. You're special."

"Me? Special? Why?" I thought of Miss Sturm and her *whys*.

"Well . . . because . . . ."

The car was still running, and I knew she was anxious to leave.

"Because is not an answer!" I said. I even sounded like Sturm!

"Because . . . you could have been *my* niece."

"Your niece! How?"

She leaned across the seat and reached for the door. "My youngest sister was contracted to marry your father." She pulled the door shut.

ELEVEN

Her niece! I felt like Lucinda in *Looking for Love* when she met her own brother who had been adopted by another family and she didn't know him when she met him at the fraternity party and didn't know they were related and . . . it wasn't a very good story. In fact, it was the only book I never finished.

As the car backed down the drive, Mrs. Enomoto cut her right turn too short, rear wheels jolting over the curb. It was probably the first mistake she'd ever made.

I walked slowly toward the house wishing I hadn't asked Mrs. Enomoto that last why. I already had enough problems figuring out who I was; now, on top of that, I was a might-have-been or maybe a supposed-to-be. Nez had told me once that I was having an identity problem. She should have seen me now.

It wasn't very late, and I didn't want to go in the house because I didn't want to talk to anyone or try to explain to anyone, but there was nowhere else to go. I was ready to open the door when a car drove up, the garage door swished, and Ernie walked toward me.

"What are you doing standing out here?"

"I'm trying to understand something." It sounded like a bad replay of my conversation with Spider the night before I left home.

"Not under*standing*, *standing* out here. Do you mean that your misunderstanding is outstanding or that your misunderstanding is understandable or maybe that you're astoundingly outstanding in your misunder . . ."

"Stop it!" I said. "This is serious." He did make me feel like laughing, but I wasn't going to.

"You should see it written in Japanese," he said. "What don't you understand? Life? Truth? Beauty? Justice? Ask me. I had an introduction to philosophy class last semester. I'll even share my Oriental wisdom."

"You're crazy," I said.

"Perceptive, very perceptive. I think I overdosed on movies. You are looking at—" he paused dramatically— "at one of the few survivors of a triple feature Kung Fu Festival."

"What are you talking about?"

He looked at me. He looked at the ground. He looked at the sky and shook his head. "Don't they have movies in Iowa? Let's start gently—at the beginning. Jujitsu?"

I nodded.

"Karate?"

I nodded.

"Tae Kwon Do?"

"Of course," I answered. "So?"

"So I have just sat through five hours of movies devoted to the martial arts."

"Why? You planning to be a samurai?" At least I knew that word, thanks to Davey and his Plan A.

"No. I'm a masochist at heart. I hate violence, so once a year I go to the movies. Last year it was Rocky. All of them. It's like knocking your head against a wall. It feels good when you stop. Isn't that what you've been doing? Running into blank walls?"

"I suppose so. But I can't understand how Mrs. Enomoto could be so . . . so sneaky. Do you know what she just told me?"

"That her sister was supposed to marry your father. That their parents had the marriage arranged."

"You knew that! How?"

"Mrs. Enomoto told me."

"When?"

"Couple of days ago. Before you went up to Tule Lake."

"Why didn't you tell me?"

"You didn't ask. Besides. . . ." He grinned a Davey grin. "It wasn't her fault it didn't work out. If it had, you wouldn't be standing here. Did you ever think of that?"

"No."

"Anyway, let's do something. Want to walk to the mall? After five hours of sitting, I need the exercise."

After my etiquette session with Mrs. Enomoto, I needed more than a walk.

"Let's run," I said.

That was the last scene in *Run for Love*. Trish and Jason hold hands and run up the mountain path to "their spot" where she collapses in his arms, and he kisses her for the first and only time in the book.

It wasn't that way with Ernie and me. Our running together turned into a race, and by the time we reached the mall, both of us nearly collapsed, and we didn't kiss, we leaned against the side of the wall, sweating. Nobody ever sweats in books.

"Hope you have some money with you," he said, after we had ordered our cokes and burgers. "Cause I haven't."

That didn't happen in books either.

He bit into the burger, ketchup dripping over his fingers. "That stuff with Mrs. Enomoto really bothering you?"

"Yes. Things like that happen in books, not in real life."

I didn't tell him what kinds of books.

He wiped the ketchup from his chin with the back of his hand. "It's really not that coincidental. There are other Yogushis in the world. Okamuras too."

"What do names have to do with anything?"

"They have to do with everything. Isn't that why you're here? Anyway, when I told Mrs. Enomoto about you, she knew the name, of course, but it wasn't until later that she made the connection. She wasn't going to tell you about that, though. She thought you had enough on your mind. Besides, it was all over a long time ago."

"She wouldn't have, but I kept asking her why she was helping me."

"Look, it doesn't make any difference to her now. Nor to you. Maybe to your father's family. Some things change; some things don't. Maybe if you find them, it won't matter at all." He sipped noisily on his straw, making annoying little gurgling sounds. "You've got to understand it was a different world back then. Tradition wasn't just a phrase. It was alive, and it controlled their lives. Things like respect, saving face weren't just words. They were ways of living. Children obeyed without question. Even grown children. You married the person your father chose. It still exists, sort of." He rested both elbows on the table and leaned toward me. "I have a friend—in her middle twenties—and she still keeps a bowing distance from her father."

"Bowing distance?"

"It means, if he is displeased with her about something and wants to speak to her, she will come to him, eyes lowered, and maintain a physical distance from him, so that if she had to bow there would be enough room to do it."

"How awful! That sounds like—"

"I know what it sounds like. It sounds like subservience. It sounds feudal, but for Emma and her father it is visible respect."

"Are you like that with your father?"

"No. The respect is there but we're assimilated—at least on the outside. You see, Kimi, whoever you are, you have to have a sense of the past. And you have to understand the present; otherwise you don't have a future. That's what you're trying to do, isn't it? To understand your past. That's why I volunteer my time at the school. It links me to my past, makes the present worthwhile and helps me face the future."

Ernie didn't sound like himself. He still had a trace of ketchup that he'd missed.

"That isn't what's worrying me now. I know it's silly, but I'm sort of scared."

"Who isn't?"

"I mean. Maybe I shouldn't try to find them. Maybe I know enough already."

"Then don't. Of course, if you don't, won't you always wonder?"

The bill was $4.57. Ernie left the tip. We didn't run home. We walked, slowly. Crossing the lawn up to the house, Ernie reached over, hugged me—a strong, warm hug—and said, "Kimi, I don't know where you're going, but I'm glad you came."

So was I.

The next morning, I stood looking at the scruffy clothes I had brought. I couldn't possibly show up at my aunt's wearing a baggy T-shirt, and I didn't need a Mrs. Enomoto to tell me that either. If I only had a decent blouse. I considered going over to the mall to buy a new one, but I was getting low on money. Where had it gone? I had insisted on paying for our breakfasts and lunches on the Tule Lake trip, and there were the taxi fares . . . and the birth certificate, a couple of lunches at the burger shop when no one was around at Barbara's, and I'd paid Barbara every time I called Davey. Oh, and that night I walked to the mall to call Davey, I'd picked up five more paperback romances, a couple of candy bars, and a pair of pink plastic spaghetti shoes that looked real California, and. . . .

Then I thought of Mom's credit card. She had given it to me "in case you want to take Mrs. Mueller out for dinner some night at the Port Inn." I remembered Davey's warning, in parentheses, of course, "Use only in an emergency." My aunt was an emergency. I'd use the credit card and worry about explaining to Mom later.

At the mall, finding the right kind of gift wrapping for the picture was a problem. Everything I looked at was covered with storks or wedding bells. Neither was appropriate. I found some plain white paper and paid cash. Looking for something to wear was even worse. Everything was either too big, too expensive, or too ridiculous. I settled for a shirt: long, red, and cheap. It looked like the leftover top from a jogging suit or maybe a pair of pajamas.

It took three times as long to get the attention of a salesperson as it did for me to find what I wanted to buy. Why, when you're in a hurry, do salespeople always seem to be busy stocking shelves or shuffling piles of paper?

"May I help you." She didn't make it a question. Maybe she was thinking about how her feet hurt or wondering whether she took the hamburger out of the freezer for the night's casserole. She looked at me as if I were a TV set with the commercial running.

I pushed the shirt across the counter.

"Cash or charge." Question marks had definitely been left out of her vocabulary.

"Charge," I said, handing her Mom's credit card.

She filled out the slip, picked up the credit card, and stopped, looking at me now as if the commercial were over and the soap had resumed. "You're Gretchen Andrews?" She had finally discovered question marks.

"No. It's my mother's card. I'm Kim Andrews."

"Are you sure?"

I wanted to say, "No, I'm not sure. That's what I'm out here trying to find out." Instead I answered. "As long as I can remember I've been."

"Do you have any identification?"

Davey hadn't thought of that. Neither had I. I dug into my purse. I didn't have my driver's license yet, but I had my plane ticket. I was about to give that to her when I remembered the ticket was made out to Kimi Yogushi. I dug deeper into my purse. There was nothing there except Miss Sturm's orange slip that I was supposed to give to Mom. It was embarrassing, but it was the only thing I had.

"Will this do?" I asked.

The woman smoothed out the wadded paper, frowning as she read. "One minute please. I'll have to get the manager's okay."

It was worse than standing outside Sturm's office waiting for another lecture. I looked down the aisle. The two women were standing with their backs to me, bent over, their shoulders shaking. It must have been five minutes before the clerk returned and, without saying anything, handed me my orange slip and ran Mom's credit card through the stamper.

"May I say, Kim," she said as she handed me my package, "you certainly are honest. Who else would use a summons from a principal? What did you do?"

"Skipped history class." I grinned.

The woman cupped one hand over her mouth and whispered, "The pits, isn't it? I did that once. Twice, really, and almost didn't graduate."

Back at Barbara's I found scissors and tape and laid them with the wrapping paper on the kitchen table. I smoothed the picture flat and looked at it. They were standing on a beach, Mom and my father, on what must have been a windy day. Mom's skirt was whipping in the ocean's breeze; Father's face was slightly out of focus. They were smiling, holding hands, and looking at each other, not at the camera.

Why had Mom saved just this one picture? Photos are scary, stopping time with a single click and holding a moment forever. Mom looked so happy and young, Father so handsome. I stared at the picture as if by some magic the two would spring to life and dash down the beach together. And then I sort of understood why Mom had kept it. They were . . . they were in love, and it wasn't like the love in any book I'd read. I folded the wrapping paper gently around the photograph.

The iron grill of the Ozaki house was open. I rang the bell and waited. I tried to peer through the beveled glass door without looking as if I were peeking. I was ten minutes early. Maybe it *was* bred in *my* genes, too. I went over what I was going to say, but I had forgotten everything Mrs. Enomoto had told me. When the door finally opened, I said the first thing that popped into my head. "Are you Mrs. Ozaki?"

She wasn't much taller than I, and there was no gray in her hair. She looked at me unsmiling, as if she were waiting for me to say something more, so I did. "I'm the person Mrs. Enomoto called about. I know I'm early, but I hope you don't mind."

She stepped back, without speaking, and motioned for me to come in. She shut the door behind me. "Then you are—?"

"Kimi," I said and hesitated. "Kimi . . . Andrews."

"We can talk in here." She turned and I followed her into a sunroom full of hanging green plants and white wicker furniture. Sitting in a chair in the corner was a tiny white-haired woman, and I knew, even before my aunt spoke, that I was seeing my grandmother

"This is my mother," my aunt said. "She does not speak English." Then she turned to the older woman, spoke in Japanese and gestured toward me. All I recognized was my name.

My grandmother looked at me, a long, steady look, then she smiled and nodded.

"Please sit down," my aunt said, politely but coolly. "Now what is it you wish from us? I'm not sure we can be of any help. I don't believe I know anyone by the name of Andrews."

I started to answer, then stopped. I wanted to say, "My name's Yogushi. You're my aunt." Instead I kept my eyes lowered and said, "Andrews isn't my real name. I'm adopted. I mean, I'm half adopted. My mother is my real mother, but my dad isn't my real father."

"*Umi-no-oya-yori mo sodate no oya,*" my grandmother said, without looking up.

"Mother says," my aunt explained, "adoptive parents are real parents. It's an old Japanese proverb."

"I thought she didn't know English," I said, forgetting again everything Mrs. Enomoto had taught me.

"She doesn't speak it. She understands a little," my aunt replied, looking at me curiously.

I felt like an intruder. As far as they were concerned, I probably *was* an intruder.

"I live in Iowa," I said, as if that explained anything.

'And you are here in California for a visit? You have family here?"

"You see," I searched for a way to explain. "My father, my real father, I mean, lived here in Sacramento . . . and in Tule. . . ."

My grandmother closed her eyes.

"Your father spoke to you of Tule Lake?" My aunt leaned forward.

"Well . . . no," I said. "He died before I was born. But I've been there. This week. Mrs. Enomoto took me."

"I don't understand, Kimi. Who exactly is Mrs. Enomoto? What is the connection? Is she a friend of your family?"

So I told them a little bit about Barbara and Ernie and the Opportunity School and how I'd met Mrs. Enomoto. Then I added, "Mrs. Enomoto was in Tule Lake when she was my age, only her name was Ochida then."

The room was quiet. Why had I said *Ochida?* Slowly my aunt stood and half turned toward the door. Grandmother spoke to her quietly but firmly. My aunt turned back to me. "Mother says we should offer you tea."

"Thank you," I said just as Mrs. Enomoto had coached me. "That would be nice." I crossed my legs at my ankles.

She left the room and I sat alone with my grandmother. I didn't know where to look. I wanted to look at her, but I didn't want to stare, although she was staring at me. I glanced around the room searching for something to talk about. Then I realized that anything I said might have been as meaningless to her as the conversation in Kai's Fountain had been to me. Our pasts were different. The language was wrong. I shouldn't have come. We could have been talking, but there weren't any words.

Finally, Grandmother motioned me toward her. I stood and took a couple of steps. She motioned again until I was near. We looked at each other for what seemed a long time. Finally she reached out and fingered the material of my new red shirt. Laughing, she spoke in Japanese, then looked up at me. "Pajama?"

"Blouse," I suggested.

She shook her head. "Not pajama. Not blouse." She tilted her head and smiled. For just a minute she reminded me of Jav and her phony French phrases. "Sweat . . . shop?"

I didn't know what she meant, and then I understood. "Sweat*shirt*," I said.

"Sweat . . . *shirt*," she repeated.

We were both laughing when my aunt came back with the tea.

The tea tray was beautiful. Not that I had seen many tea trays, but I knew she had spent time preparing and arranging the linen napkins, rice and ginger sweets, baby's-breath blooms, and hand-painted cups as thin as eggshells.

It was as if my aunt had changed, or maybe it was impolite to ask serious questions and drink tea at the same time. Instead she asked about Iowa, about my school, and about my flight to California. She did not mention Tule Lake or the name Ochida. Neither did I.

After we were finished with our tea, my aunt took the tray to the kitchen, came back and stood in the doorway. "You've lived all your life in Iowa then?"

"Yes," I answered, wondering where that question was going to lead.

"You came to find out about Tule Lake? About your father at Tule Lake? You know your father's name, of course?"

"Yes."

Then I did what I vowed I would never do again. I unbridled my intelligence. That was what Dad said lying was—unbridled intelligence.

"You see. . . ." I took a deep breath. "I'm doing research . . . for a history term paper . . . on my father. He was Japanese. . . . And my mom said my father used to have a good friend out here. . . ." I was talking too fast again. "A good friend named Yogushi and I thought . . . and Mrs. Enomoto thought, too . . . that you might have known him . . . or something. Maybe about him or if he might have been a neighbor or something because Mom told me that. . . ."

My aunt stared at me and shook her head. "Your mother said. . . ?"

"Oh, Mom. She's Irish. Not like me."

Now I was telling the truth again and getting confused,

174

but not nearly as confused as my aunt looked. Mrs. Eno-moto would have fainted.

There was nothing for me to do but get out and get out fast. I looked frantically toward the door, measuring the number of leaps it would take to escape. I stood, my face burning. "I have to go now. I've got to catch a plane. Thank you for the tea." And I fled.

Running down the steps, I remembered that I hadn't left the gift. I hadn't closed the door either. I rushed back in. My aunt was standing in the middle of the room looking as if she couldn't believe what she was seeing. I yanked the wrapped picture from my purse, dropped it into my grandmother's lap, and ran.

My ears stung as if they were frostbitten, and my mouth had a nasty, dry taste as I climbed on my bike and pedaled as fast as I could from a family I was somehow afraid to claim.

Why was I doing what I was doing? It didn't make sense to me, and I was the one who was doing it. I swore I'd never ask *why* about anything again. *Why* supposed there had to be reasons. Sometimes you do things just because you feel like it, for no reason at all. The crazy thing is that it's harder to answer your own *whys* than someone else's. So why did I lie? Why did I make a complete fool of myself? And why didn't I tell them who I was? I made a list of answers, something like Nez's checklist. Basically lacks moral fiber. That was for lying.

Immature in decision-making. That was for acting like an idiot. The last question was hardest, just the way it always is on a test. Why didn't I tell them? I knew what the answer was. I guess I'd known for a long time. What if I'd told them who I was and they didn't care?

I was a Hapa all right, and I was going to "hop" right out of Sacramento and back to Lanesport, whether I belonged there or not.

TWELVE

I wheeled the bicycle into the garage. I certainly wouldn't be needing it again. I was headed for my room when Barbara stuck her head out of the den.

"You look as if you need to cool down."

"I do. I'm going to take a shower," I said.

"Good. When you've finished, go out to the pool. I'll bring some iced tea. Ernie's there with a friend."

I never wanted to taste tea, hot or cold, again.

"Wonderful," I lied. Lying isn't really lying when you know you're doing it. At least you're not lying to yourself, because you know you're doing it, and that's being honest —kind of honest, anyway.

I stood in the shower for at least ten minutes. When I was little, Mom read me a story about a mother cat teaching her kittens how to survive out in the world. "When in doubt, bathe," the mother cat told them. I wasn't sure whether I was washing away my doubts or my dreams.

I got dressed and ran a comb through my damp hair. The person looking back at me from the mirror was exactly the same person as yesterday, last week, last year. She was Kimi Yogushi. How could my aunt and grandmother not have recognized me? Of course, they weren't expecting me, but . . . and I wasn't looking forward to talking to Ernie, either, or to meeting his friend, but I couldn't be impolite after everything he and his mother had done for me.

I headed for the pool. Ernie was stretched out on the diving board, and near him, in the chaise longue, back toward me, was his friend, long legs extended.

"Hi," I said in my best, won't-this-be-fun voice. I hoped it didn't sound too phony.

A rich, throaty contralto sang, "We three kings of Orient are, bearing gifts we travel afar. *And* I'm the gift!" Jav poked her head around the corner of the chaise.

"I don't believe it! This is unreal," I shouted.

"If you think this is unreal, you should have been on that flight from Denver. We didn't fly here. We bounced." Jav untangled her legs and pulled a chair up next to her for me.

As I collapsed, Jav stuck her arm out in front of me. "Touch, Kim, touch. See, I'm real and I'm here. You're making me think I'm some figment of your imagination. It would help if you'd close your mouth."

I closed my mouth, then I opened it again. "Ernie," I began.

Jav reached over and poked him in the ribs. "Ernie's real, too. In fact," she went on, winking at me, "Ernie's really real!"

"But how'd you get here?"

"Ernie met me at the airport. He's a much better driver than our pilot was. Cuter too," she added.

Ernie sat up and swung around facing us. "Kimi, I've decided to quit college and go into the import-escort business. Importing Iowans and escorting them around Sacramento."

"He's just kidding, Kim. He's not quitting college. I'm coming out here to the university next fall."

"When did you decide that?"

"Five minutes ago."

"Why?"

"Why not? I'm going to major in marine biology. I'm intrigued by the local fauna."

"But he's too short for you, Jav," I said, forgetting Ernie was listening.

Jav stood up, grabbed Ernie's hand, and tugged him into the pool. "No he isn't," she said as they bobbed in the deep water. "See. In our natural element, we're exactly the same size."

"If you don't stop it, right now," I said, "I'm going to—"

Just then Barbara came out with the tea.

"What are you going to do?" Barbara asked.

"Drink my tea," I said.

"I wanted to tell you," Barbara explained, "but your friend Jav said that you loved surprises."

"Adore them." I crunched an ice cube between my back teeth.

Barbara pulled up another chair, Jav and Ernie pulled themselves out of the pool, and I tried to pull my thoughts together.

"Look." I turned to Jav, trying to look angry. "Why. . . ." I stopped and thought of my promise to myself. "I mean *how* did you find out where I was staying? And why aren't you in Colorado, falling down ski slopes?"

"That's easy," Jav said. "I blackmailed my parents by threatening to repeat my senior year. They decided they'd save their sanity by letting me fly out here instead. And fly home with you," she added with a sort of grim emphasis.

"Now *you're* sounding like the milk carton. That's another half and half. In *this* case, half an answer. How did you know where to find me?"

"Oh, that." Jav wrapped a towel around her shoulders. She could always do things like that, throw a towel or a sweater around herself and look like something out of a high-fashion magazine. When I tried it, I always looked as if I were escaping from a burning building.

"Oh, *that*," I repeated. "How *did* you know?"

Barbara and Ernie looked as if they were watching the finals of an Olympic volleyball game.

"Mrs. Mueller, of course," Jav answered. "But more important, what was your aunt like? You went to see her this afternoon, didn't you?"

Now all three of them were looking at me.

"Your aunt!" Barbara choked on her tea.

"You found her!" Ernie shouted.

"How did *you* know, Jav? How could you know?"

Then I answered my own question. "Mrs. Mueller, of course."

"Mrs. Mueller, of course," Jav repeated. "I talked to her this morning before I left Colorado, and she said that Davey said that you told him over the phone yesterday that you were going to meet your aunt."

Then the questions came. It was worse than being grilled by Sturm. I'd just answer one question and then there'd be another. I didn't even have time to lie.

"And that's when I left." I finished the story.

"Without telling them who you were?" I thought Barbara was going to levitate out of her chair.

"I think they might have a good idea by now, though," I muttered.

"How?" Jav, if we'd been alone, would have added a nasty-sounding French phrase.

"Because I left the picture."

"What picture?" Ernie exclaimed.

"Of Mom and my father."

"Cool! Really intelligent." Jav looked up and rolled her eyes. "You probably gave your grandmother a heart attack."

Barbara looked at Ernie. Ernie looked back at his mother. "Of all the un-Japanese things you could have done!" Barbara broke out laughing. "You chose a winner. What did they say?"

"I didn't wait to find out."

Barbara held her head. Ernie slipped back into the pool. Jav stood up, towering over me. "You certainly blew it, Yum-Yum. What are you going to do now?"

"Go home, I guess. If there's a flight out tonight."

"We can't! I've got a hotel room and three credit cards."

"You're welcome to stay here," Barbara broke in. "I have an extra futon."

"That's very nice, Mrs. Okamura, but my parents made a reservation for me, and they're going to call me tonight to see if I checked in. Anyway, I'm going to need a place to recuperate after what's going to happen next." Jav sat down again.

"And what's that?" I asked, not really wanting to know.

"Well, obviously, weed-brain, you're getting ready to try out for the track team. Do you want me to be your trainer?"

"What do you mean?"

"Running. You're really getting pretty good at running. Most of the time, though, you're going in the wrong direction. You've got to go back. You've got to talk to them again. You've got to finish what you've started."

I looked at Ernie. I looked at Barbara. Neither one came to my rescue.

"Jav's probably right, but they will need time to talk," Barbara said. "After all, it will be a shock to them. Your grandmother, whether she was happy to see you or not, will probably feel tied to the past—to your grandfather's decision. Your aunt? Well, she's younger. A different generation. She may accept you. Even welcome you."

I was sure Barbara was wrong. If I were welcomed at all, it would be by my grandmother.

"In any case, you must let them get in touch with you, now," Barbara went on. "Do they know you're staying here?"

"No," I said. "But they'd get in touch with Mrs. Enomoto. She called for me."

"There's nothing you can do about it now." Ernie stood up and draped his towel around his shoulders. "I'll get dressed and take you two over to the hotel so Jav can check in. When you're ready to come back, give me a call."

"Yes," Barbara agreed. "But do come back. We'll have dinner here and see what happens."

It sounded like a fine idea to me. I couldn't wait to get Jav off by herself. I had several important questions to ask that she hadn't answered.

Jav won the bet. On the way to the hotel, she'd assured me that the room would be either ecru and orange, ecru and brown, or ecru and aqua. I picked brown; she chose orange.

"See, I told you," Jav said as she closed the door. "You owe me a pizza when we get home."

"You owe me a lot more than that," I said.

"What's that?"

"Some answers."

"Okay, okay. But let me unpack first."

Jav took a long time unpacking a very small suitcase. Finally she finished and flopped across the bed. "That's why I came."

"What's why you came?"

"What you want to ask me. You see, I didn't cover for you. I uncovered. I was having a perfectly lousy time in Colorado, anyway. I'm a fink. I'm a rat. I'm a Sturm. I didn't send an orange slip to your parents, but I did tell Mrs. Mueller. And I'd like to feel absolutely rotten about it, but you know what?" She sat up, cross-legged on the bed, and grinned at me. "I don't."

"*You* told Mrs. Mueller even before I left Lanesport! It *wasn't* Davey! But you promised!" I was shouting. "I thought you were my friend!"

"I didn't really promise, and I am your friend. That's why I couldn't let you come by yourself. There're so many awful things that could have happened. Stuff you read in the paper every day."

"When?" I asked.

"When what?"

"When did you tell Mrs. Mueller."

"That same afternoon you told me. After you left Davey at her house."

"I saw the *Pink Passion* when I was walking home. Why didn't you tell me that night?"

"Would that have stopped you?" Jav looked at me seriously.

"No. But I sure wouldn't have waited around to meet Mrs. Mueller's Celia the Serene."

"I know. That's why I didn't tell you. Besides it worked out all right, didn't it?"

"I suppose so," I admitted. "In a way it made everything easier."

"Just one other thing." She crawled off the bed and started fiddling with the air conditioning. "Davey and I . . . well . . . Davey and I and Mrs. Mueller . . . we talked it over and we . . . we. . . ." She turned to face me. "We called your parents in Chicago that night."

"You didn't!" I fell across the bed, face down. I bounced up again. "Then they knew! They knew I was coming out here even before I left the airport back home?"

"Something like that." Jav headed for the bathroom. "I'm going to take a shower."

"Everybody told everybody then," I shouted after her.

Jav peeked around the door. "They're going to meet us at the airport tomorrow. They came back early."

"What am I going to do?" I was almost screaming.

"I imagine you're going to grow up. Quick! Make a

guess, Kim. When your folks found out, guess who said, 'Stop her. We'll catch the next plane home'?"

"Both of them," I answered.

"Nope. Neither one."

"Honest?"

"Yep. And who do you think said, 'Let her go. It's a trip she must take'?"

"Both of them?"

"Obviously."

My stomach felt like crying.

"Do you think? Do you suppose?" I couldn't put it into words. "I mean . . . I hurt them, didn't I?"

"They must love you very much. And trust you to do whatever you have to do. I guess that's what being a real mother and father is."

I sat down on the edge of the bed. "Go take your shower," I muttered.

I wished I were home in my own bedroom, propped up in bed with a stack of my books in reaching distance. I'd probably reread *Victory for Vikki*, that part when she smiles at herself in the mirror just before she goes on stage in the beauty pageant and she says . . . I couldn't remember what she said. I tried thinking about another book, *Caring for Carrie*. That was the one where the girl overcame a lisp. No. That wasn't right. That was the one . . . I gave up.

Then I started thinking about the people I'd seen the

past week: the Bisignano woman who helped me with the phone books, the old man with the long white beard sitting at the bus stop, Mr. Verenzo and his sad dog, Mrs. Enomoto. I would never have met them in any book. They weren't young. They didn't have pretty eyes, shiny teeth, and lovely hair. But they were real.

I stared at the bathroom door. Jav was real, too, and I was so glad to see her. Funny, but I wasn't quite as scared now about going home and facing Mom and Dad. They had understood me better than I had. But the one face that I kept seeing was my grandmother's, when we had laughed together. I had spoiled any chance of our understanding each other.

I walked over to the dresser. Jav's plane ticket was lying there. The plane left the next day at two. I looked at my watch. Five-thirty. Jav had been right, in a way. I had been running, running around in circles. It was time I stopped to see if standing still could work any better. I'd go back home and let my Japanese family find me, if they wanted to, but first there was something I had to do: call Mrs. Enomoto and thank her for all she had done for me. I wouldn't lie, but if she asked me how the visit went, I'd say "All right." It was a handy expression that could mean almost anything.

By the time Jav got out of the shower, I had bumbled my way through the phone call, answering all Mrs. Enomoto's questions with "I think so" and "Maybe," and had called the airport to reserve a seat on the plane home. My quest was over. Davey's fantasy game was ended, and I was no longer Sybil the Seeker.

After dinner at Barbara's, we sat on the patio, watching the color fade from the sky. I wondered if Spider had returned my bike wheel in one piece, if Jeffrey were still around Lanesport, and if Davey had managed to wiggle out of his part in our Plan A. Most of all, I wondered what I'd say to Mom and Dad. Whatever it was, it would be the truth . . . I hoped.

The doorbell rang and, before Ernie could answer it, it rang again and again.

"Helen!" Barbara stood up.

I turned. It was Mrs. Enomoto. I had never thought of her having a first name.

"Come. Sit down and join us." Barbara motioned toward a chair. "This is Kimi's friend Jav from Iowa."

Mrs. Enomoto nodded at Jav, but she looked at me. She didn't sit down. "Did you hear from Kimi's aunt?" Barbara asked the question I was hoping she wouldn't ask.

"I *certainly* did!" Mrs. Enomoto walked over to me.

I edged my chair back to what I thought was an appropriate bowing distance. "What did she say?" I asked, keeping my eyes lowered. I hoped she noticed that I had remembered at least one thing she had told me.

"A great deal more than you told me."

"Kim condenses her stories, sometimes," Jav suggested.

It sounded ever so much better than saying I lied.

"I . . . I didn't. . . ." I began and started over. "I didn't want to upset you after all you'd taught me."

"You didn't upset me, but you certainly made an impression on your aunt and grandmother. What kind, I'm not sure. However, they are willing to see you again, but. . . ." Mrs. Enomoto paused.

I waited for what was to follow the *but*. *But* was right up there with Sturm's *why*.

"But what time does your plane leave?" she went on.

"Two." I was down to one-syllable answers.

"Good. They will expect you late in the morning. Somehow they were under the impression that you had already left."

I didn't have even a one-syllable answer for that.

"Are they going to own me or disown me?" I managed a question.

"I'm not sure." Mrs. Enomoto finally laughed. "But at least they know who you are now."

"I sure bungled it, didn't I?"

"The understatement of the year," Jav mumbled.

"You have to break eggs to make an omelet," Ernie said. "It's an old Japanese saying." He winked at his mother.

"At least, Kimi, you were original." Mrs. Enomoto was still standing.

I kept wishing she'd sit down. I had to keep looking up at her, even though she wasn't that tall, and my neck was getting stiff.

"Eleven tomorrow morning, Kimi. Your grandmother usually takes a short morning nap, but they will be expecting you."

"What'll I do this time?" I didn't want to go back again. I didn't want another lesson in Japanese etiquette, either. I wished I hadn't asked the question in the first place.

"Play it by ear," Ernie suggested.

"Kim's got a tin ear." Jav sipped on her iced tea. I gave her a dirty look, but she wouldn't look at me.

Mrs. Enomoto finally turned from me and spoke to Ernie. "I'm sure Kimi will handle the situation nicely. You'll see."

Mrs. Enomoto left at last. Barbara disappeared into the den. Ernie took Jav back to her hotel, and I sat on my futon and thought about my tomorrow. *My Tomorrow!* That was it! That was the name of the book I was trying to remember, the one about the girl who wore braces and lisped.

THIRTEEN

I wheeled the Schwinn out of the garage—again. I looked down at the muscles in my legs. Maybe I'd go on one of those bicycle rides with Spider when I got home. Ernie and Jav would have driven me to my aunt's, but I wanted to go by myself. I'd had too much help already. This was one thing I had to do alone.

Barbara offered me something different to wear, but I'd washed out my red "sweat shop" the night before. It was a little faded, a little wrinkled, a little smaller, but it was mine. In fact, the only things that weren't mine were the bicycle and the family I was about to meet again.

Pedaling down the driveway and into the empty street, I decided that whatever happened it would have to be because of me, not because of my father or Mrs. Enomoto's sister or because of a grandfather I'd never known. My aunt and my grandmother would be meeting *me*. That's when I made the big decision, just as I caught sight of my aunt's house. *Me* was Kimi Yogushi Andrews. From now on I would be Kimi Y. Andrews. It was different. It had color. It was *me*.

And it was *my* aunt, opening the heavy glass door before I even rang the bell.

At first I didn't feel anything except frozen as if I really were trapped in one of Davey's magic spells. Maybe my aunt felt that way too because she stood for a long time looking at me. We might as well have been a photograph, like the one I had left them yesterday.

Finally, I lowered my eyes and made a kind of stiff, awkward half bow. I didn't know if bowing to an aunt was proper, but I was sure it couldn't be as impolite as what I'd done the day before. It must have been all right because she said, "Come in, Kimi." I followed her to the same green-and-white room. Grandmother's chair was empty. My aunt sat down, but I stood waiting until she motioned me to a chair. I waited for her to speak again.

After all the running and searching and the mistakes of the past week, everything now was happening in slow motion. I'd seen so many places, talked to so many people, asked myself so many questions that the silence and slowness was somehow peaceful rather than awkward.

"You are my brother's daughter." Her words were neither happy nor sad and it wasn't a question, so I decided that she wasn't expecting an answer. "Neither my mother nor I knew you existed. We never met. . . ," she hesitated, "your mother."

Still looking at the floor, I answered as quietly as I could. "She wrote to you, to your mother and father, but the letter came back."

"My father. How can I explain? You have to understand *him* to know. Born in Japan, he came over as a young man, prospered, but was never allowed by the government here to become an American citizen. Then came the war. Can you see?"

"I think so."

"Mother was a picture bride, the marriage arranged in Japan. My father met her for the first time when she got off the boat. She was from his own province. Much younger."

I looked up. "You mean they married without knowing each other?"

"It had been arranged. That is why Kenji . . . my brother was . . . but we'll talk about that later. That was very painful for my parents. Father was a product of thousands of years of Japanese culture. Strict Buddhist, descendant of a samurai, but you can't really understand what all that means, can you?"

"No," I said. "That's why I wanted to find you. To find out about my father and my family. To find out about the part of me that I have never known."

"And the finding? Has it been as surprising and as . . . as painful as it has been for us?"

"I didn't mean to hurt you," I hurried to explain. "I wasn't sure you'd want to know me. I guess that's why I acted so awful yesterday. I was afraid."

My aunt smoothed her dress across her lap with the palms of her hands and sighed. It wasn't a sad sigh. It was more as if she were catching her breath. "I suppose we were afraid, too, my mother and I, after we saw the picture. Afraid of reliving the past. Afraid of remembered pain. Afraid of the same old sorrows. I think, though, my mother was not so surprised. You look very much like my brother. I see it now."

"Have I made her unhappy? Doesn't she want to see me?"

"She needs time. Kenji's action caused our family to, what Father called, 'lose face.' My mother had no choice but to obey his decision."

"Even after he died?" I asked, trying not to raise my voice.

"Yes. Until now. Until you. After you left yesterday, we talked. We talked far into the night and on into the morning. We said things to each other that had been left unsaid for much too long."

"I think I know what you mean." For the last three or four years I had been feeling things, thinking things, doing things and never sharing with Mom and Dad. Maybe they had wanted to say things to me, too, and couldn't.

"Kimi, there is so much of the past that is not *your* past."

"You mean the camps."

"That. But more than that. Everything that led to them. The whole Japanese-American heritage. The rules. The tradition. All so strange, so alien, to American thought. My mother was part of it. I'm the result of it. And you...."

"I'm a Hapa. A Sansei-Hapa, and I think that's important."

She did not answer. I had expected to be hugged and welcomed by my aunt and grandmother or else ignored. Neither was happening.

"But you don't know how to be either one. Am I right?"

"I suppose. That's why I tried to find you. To learn. I didn't want anything from you. Just the knowing that there was somebody I belonged to. Besides Mom and Dad, I mean."

She looked out the window, her head tilted on one hand, her profile a silhouette against the light. I thought about what Ernie had told me, on that walk home from the mall, about the pencil test. I thought he was putting me on when he told me that we Japanese couldn't open our eyes if we laid a pencil across the bridge of our nose. Neither my aunt nor I could have passed the pencil test.

"I'm not doing this very well, Kimi. I don't have children of my own. I'm not used to talking with young people."

"I think you're doing just fine." I grinned. She was, too. She was every bit as good as Sturm, who spent all day, every day, talking to kids. And what my aunt had to say was a lot more interesting. "You're better than I was yesterday," I added.

"Forgive me for saying so, but almost anyone would have been more coherent yesterday. I didn't understand half the things you were saying."

"Neither did I," I admitted, "but I thought if I talked fast enough, you wouldn't notice."

She laughed. At first she covered her mouth so that I thought she was yawning because she was tired or bored, but then I saw that she was trying to hide her laughing. Then she didn't bother to hide it. "You *are* like my brother." She took a deep breath. "Like your father. Like Kenji. He had only two bad habits. Sometimes he didn't tell the complete truth and sometimes he spoke too quickly. Most often he did both at the same time. And Father always knew."

I glanced down at my watch. My aunt saw me.

"Your plane?"

"It leaves at two."

"Time is getting short."

"I know."

"It's not really, though. It's all ahead for you. Mother's time stretches behind her." She looked away. "Her tomorrows, like her memory of yesterdays, do not come easily . . . if at all."

I waited for her to go on.

"I can't be sure she will see you. You must try to understand what she is going through. Kenji disobeyed his father, married a Caucasian, was disowned. It is hard for Mother to go against Father's wishes, even now, and claim you as part of the family."

"Is that what she's doing? Deciding whether to claim me or not?"

"Yes." She spoke so softly I hardly heard her.

"I thought she was taking a nap."

"I wonder if you realize what a painful decision it will be for her if she decides to acknowledge you as her granddaughter."

I felt like running, but I didn't. I waited. I had run out of questions. I had run out of answers. I had run out of words. The only sound was the ticking of a clock somewhere in another room. I didn't know whether I wanted time to hurry up, so I could leave, or whether I wanted it to slow down, so I could stay. I tried to remember the rest of the plot of *My Tomorrow*, but all I could think about was a phrase from one of Barbara's books: "As children in the camps we learned, like Anne Frank, to be quiet and wait."

I looked up. My aunt was watching me, but when she saw me looking at her, she glanced away. Why couldn't she understand the way I felt? Why couldn't she accept me? Why couldn't she understand my silence?

"On the other hand. . . ." My aunt began as if she were not aware of the long pause. "Discovering a granddaughter should be a joy."

I couldn't have agreed more.

"You are all that's left of our family. I'm glad you found us, Kimi, no matter what Mother decides."

"I am, too," I said.

She stood, looked around the room, and then at me again.

"You could—perhaps—call me *obasan*. It means—aunt."

I tried to look at her, but I couldn't.

"What Kenji did was right. I know that now. My marriage was arranged, too. Shall we write? It may be easier to get to know each other through words on paper."

"We will write, *obasan*," I said, looking down at her feet. She was wearing pink plastic spaghetti shoes like the pair I had bought!

"Nomi!" Grandmother called from the next room.

"Wait." My aunt touched my arm as she hurried by.

I didn't want to wait. I wanted it all to end. I couldn't think of anything more to say. I couldn't think of anything more to feel. I couldn't think of anything to think.

I glanced at my watch again and stood up. At least my aunt would see I was ready to leave when she came back. I looked around the room, memorizing every piece of furniture, every picture, every lamp.

Finally my aunt returned—alone.

"Mother said to give you this as a gift." She handed me an envelope.

"For me? What is it?"

"I don't know."

"Shall I open it now?"

"If you like."

I opened the envelope and took out a picture—a picture of a little boy, bundled up in a homemade coat, a numbered tag on his lapel. He was standing in front of an American flag.

I felt my aunt draw near. "Kenji!" she whispered. "I didn't know Mother had this. Father made us destroy everything that belonged to my brother. She must have hidden this."

"Will she let me see her?"

My aunt rested her hand on my shoulder. "She cannot, Kimi. Not yet. It is too soon for her—too soon and too late."

I put the picture back into the envelope, trying to pretend the words didn't hurt. "Well . . . thank her for the picture anyway."

"I haven't finished. If your mother and father are willing, you must come back to visit us when your school year ends. Your grandmother says she needs time. Time to understand the past. Time to think about the future and her Kimiko."

"Kimiko?"

"It means 'her child Kimi.' It means you are family."

I walked toward the beveled glass door. The lawn dipped down to the street where Barbara's bike stood propped by the curb. I paused, my hand on the doorknob. I saw, reflected in the glass, my aunt in her pink shoes and, standing a little behind her, my Japanese grandmother, who would not speak English.

I did not turn around. I would learn to wait. After all, I *was* a Yogushi—half Yogushi, that is.

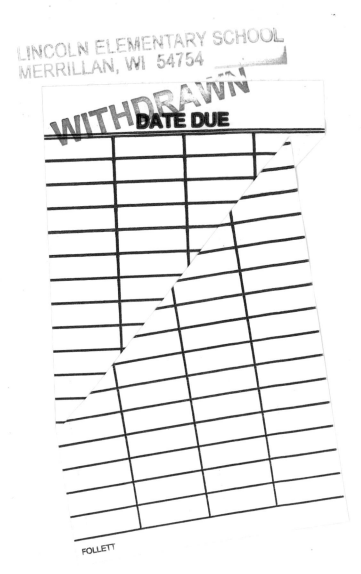

DATE DUE

FOLLETT